From Geek to Goddess

Distributed in Canada by H. B. Fenn and Company Ltd.

Library of Congress Cataloging-in-Publication Data
has been applied for.

ISBN: 978-0-7534-6323-9

Kingfisher books are available for special promotions and premiums.
For details contact: Director of Special Markets, Holtzbrinck Publishers.

Printed in the United Kingdom
10 9 8 7 6 5 4 3 2 1
1TR/0109/MCK/(SC)/60HLM/C

Zodiac Girls

From Geek to Goddess

Cathy Hopkins

KINGFISHER
NEW YORK

Chapter One

Blubber . . . blubber

"Goodbye, life." I sighed as I looked down from my bedroom window toward the bus stop at the end of the street.

Everyone was there. All my friends. Lucy. Chloe. Ellie. Jess. Charlotte. They were messing around, laughing and shoving each other as usual. *There's been some almighty humongous mistake. This* so *isn't right.* I should have been with them. I should have been *going* with them. A new start for all of us, into eighth grade.

I stared down at Jess, willing her to look up. She was my best friend, but she'd probably be Charlotte's from now on. I bet she would. She'd soon forget me. It was bound to happen if we went to different schools. She'd said that she'd wave to me from the bus stop, and she hadn't even looked up. Not once. She'd been too busy laughing with Charlotte. Instead of me. *Not going to cry, not going to cry*, I told myself as the bus came rattling down the road and Jess stuck her hand out to wave it down. It was too late—tears stung the back of my eyes, and I knew I was going to blubber. Again.

I watched my friends get on the bus and disappear off around the corner. And now the street was empty. I was alone.

Well, almost. Bertie, who had been standing, watching with me, paws up on the windowsill, looked up at me sympathetically and let out a soft whine.

I ruffled his black silky head. "And soon I'll have to say goodbye to you, too." I sighed as I turned away from the window.

My suitcase was ready on the bed. Mom had packed it for me over the weekend. New clothes. New uniform. Everything I'd need for my new school. I shoved it off the bed and onto the floor, where it landed with a loud thud.

"Well, *that's* what I think of you," I said as I stuck out my tongue at the offending case.

I took a quick glance at myself in the mirror. A huge zit stared back.

"Go away," I said to it, but it took no notice and glared back at me defiantly. I'd been lucky so far—I never usually got zits, but this one appeared over the weekend to make up for all the months without. Right in the middle of my forehead. If there was a prize for pimples, I'd win it hands down. You couldn't miss it, no matter how much concealer I plastered on. And it was one of those that you couldn't pop; it was an under-the-skin, lumpy one that just glistened red and shouted, *Whee,*

LOOK AT ME! Just what you needed on the first day of school when you want to look your best. Not.

"Yuck," I said as I made a face at myself and pulled my hair back into a ponytail. Big mistake. It only showed off my Award-Winning Zit more. *Maybe I should get bangs?* I wondered as I pulled my hair loose again. Even my hair was misbehaving today. I so wished that I had straight, blond, fine hair like Jess's and Lucy's, but no, I had a mass of boring, brown, kinky hair. I'd tried straightening it, but it had still managed to get curly again. *Great impression I'm going to make. I look like a geek. A pimply geek.*

"Gemma, Gem*MA*," Mom called up the stairs. "Almost time."

I felt a sinking feeling in the pit of my stomach. This was almost it. Goodbye to my friends. My dog. My cozy bedroom. My life.

I took off my nightgown and put on the uniform that was hanging ready on the back of the door. Prison outfit, more like. Black skirt, cream blouse, yellow-and-black tie. I took another look in the mirror, hoping that by some miracle in the last five minutes I had turned into Britney Spears and looked like a hot babe, like she did when she wore a school uniform in that old video of hers. No such luck.

"Don't call us," I said to my reflection. "We'll call you."

Mom had bought the uniform too big so that I

could grow into it—only by the look of it, that's not going to happen until around senior year. I looked ridiculous. Anyone could see that the sleeves were too long and the shoulders hung off me. I might be going to a ritzy school with ritzy girls, but my parents had to scrimp and save so that I could attend. A new uniform for me every year wasn't an option. *I bet none of the other girls have had to get a uniform that they can grow into*, I thought. *I bet all their parents are so stinking rich that they can have a new uniform every week if they want. It's so not fair. I don't want to be going to a snobby school with snobby students. I want to be going to the school with my friends, where you don't have to wear a uniform at all.*

The trouble started last summer when some ancient great aunt left some money to my parents in her will. With one condition—that the money was to be used for "a private education" for me. Mom and Dad were on cloud nine, even though there was one small problem. She hadn't left *quite* enough to cover all the tuition. Only two thirds of what was needed. That didn't stop them. They decided that "fate" had given me a chance, and they were going to do all they could to make it happen. Mom got an evening job teaching English as a foreign language on top of her normal job at the library, and Dad started putting in extra hours at his garage. All so I could go to private school.

"What a *lucky* girl you are," everyone said.

"Opportunity of a *lifetime*," I heard over and over again.

No one asked me what I wanted. What I wanted was to kill that aunt. Only she was already dead. On the rare occasions that I dared to object to being separated from my friends, Mom and Dad laughed and said that I'd soon make new ones. They *really* don't understand what changing schools can be like.

I tried getting Dad on his own, but he said that I had to remember the sacrifices that Mom was making for me.

I tried getting Mom alone, but she said that I had to remember the sacrifices that Dad was making for me.

I tried my grandparents, and Grandma said that I was in danger of becoming a "spoiled little brat."

Only Bertie understood.

And so I was off to Avebury, a new school where I knew I wouldn't belong. I hoped that when Mom and Dad saw me cast out as an outsider and failing all of my classes they would remember the sacrifices that *I* made by giving up my friends and going along with it, just to keep them happy. I had no choice in the end. What with them working all hours and wearing themselves out to give me what they thought was the "opportunity of a lifetime," I couldn't say too much. I didn't want to be seen as a "spoiled little brat."

By now I was feeling quite sorry for myself, so I opened the closet, walked in, sat on the floor, and closed the door. *Maybe if I stay here long enough,* I thought, *the back will fall through like it did in those C. S. Lewis books, and I'll find myself in a magical land like Narnia.* I knocked on the wall behind the clothes. No such luck. There was no secret door there. Only the back of the closet. I knew it was a silly thought.

Outside there was a scratching sound and a soft growl. I opened the door, and Bertie leaped in to sit on my knee. I think he knew that something was up. He'd sat in my suitcase last night as Mom packed the last things, and he refused to move until she shoved him out. He hated it when the cases came out. He knew from when we'd been on vacation that clothes being packed meant that someone was going away.

This time, it was no vacation.

"It's *so* not fair," I said to Bertie as he licked my face in the dark. "Why did that stupid aunt have to die and leave me money anyway? She'd never even met me. Maybe she was miserable all her life and wanted to make sure that someone kept suffering after she'd gone. Why couldn't she have left me the money and said, Spend it all on clothes? Now *that* would have been worth having."

"Woof," said Bertie, and he began to make himself

comfortable in my lap. Since he's a Border collie, he's not a huge dog, so it wasn't too bad, but I did feel a bit squashed all the same. Not that I minded. His warmth and familiar doggy smell were reassuring.

"Gemma, GEMMA," Mom called again, and I heard her footsteps coming up the stairs.

"Shhh," I said to Bertie as we heard my bedroom door open.

"Gemma?" asked Mom's voice.

Unfortunately, Bertie woofed in response, and a moment later, Mom opened the closet door.

"What on earth are you doing in there?" she asked as I looked up at her from behind the hems of hanging skirts and pants.

"Nothing," I replied. "Looking for Narnia."

Mom stared at me quizzically. "Narnia? Well, if it was on our list, I'd have packed it. Come on, come out. It's almost time for us to go."

I decided to make one last bid for freedom. I fell on my knees in front of her. "Mom, please, save me from this terrible fate . . ."

Mom started laughing.

Why does everyone always think it's so hysterical when I'm being deadly serious?

"I know it's a new start," said Mom as she sat on the end of my bed, "but you'll love it when you've settled in."

"Won't," I said as I sat up.

"Of course you will. You'll make new friends in no time."

"Won't. Don't want new friends. I want to be with Lucy, Chloe, Ellie, Jess, and Charlotte. They're my friends."

"You can still see them when you're home during your break. Come on, Gemma—this isn't like you. You're a very lucky girl. Avebury is one of the best schools in the country. Lots of girls would love to have this chance."

"Don't care. Don't want to go."

Mom laughed again. "See if you can stick out your bottom lip just a little bit more . . ."

"Hmpf," I replied. "No one *ever* takes me seriously."

Suddenly, Mom sighed. "Look, Gemma. I'm not having this conversation again. We've been through it a million times."

"Yeah, but no one asked me what I wanted. I wanted to go to the same school as my friends. That's a good school, too. I would be happy there."

"We only want what's best for you. This is—"

"I know," I said. "The opportunity of a lifetime. Only my life is over. Please, Mom, please. Let me go with my friends. I'll work really hard. We should all be starting eighth grade together today, and instead . . ." I felt tears welling up again. "Instead . . . I'm going to be all by myself. I won't know anyone."

"You'll know Sara Jenkins. She goes there."

I snorted. Mom didn't really know Sara. She lived in a swanky house on the next street and thought that she was God's gift. Okay, so she had long blond hair and was really pretty, but she was mean. During Christmas vacation, Jess and I saw her and her friends at the skating rink outside the town hall. It was our first time ice-skating, and when we fell over, she thought it was hilarious. She pointed at us and laughed. She, of course, had been skating for years and probably had a private instructor.

"Sara Jenkins probably already has a bunch of friends," I said. "She won't even give me a second glance."

"Well, there'll be plenty of other girls in your position, Gem. You're probably not the only person who will be starting today. Everyone's bound to be nervous, but you'll pal up with people in no time."

"Huh," I said and folded my arms. "People make friends in seventh grade when everyone is starting. By eighth grade, everyone's got their friends. The groups are fixed. The cool kids. The geeks. The computer whizzes. The nerds. The jocks. You don't understand how it works."

Mom stood up. "Now don't be childish, Gemma. You're thirteen years old and about to start at one of the best boarding schools in the country. You should count your blessings. So, enough. It's time for you to start behaving like a young lady. Now finish getting dressed and start acting your age."

I lay on my back. "Huh," I said again. "You really *don't* understand."

"Five minutes," said Mom. "And get up off that floor. Your uniform will be covered in dust."

"Good," I said. "That's how I like it."

Mom rolled her eyes and took a card out of her pocket. "By the way, your dad left this for you before he went to work this morning."

When she'd left, I ripped open the envelope. Inside was a card with a black-and-white photo of an athlete holding a huge silver cup. Inside, it said, "Winners never quit and quitters never win. So get out there, walk tall, and show them what you can do. Love, Dad."

My eyes filled with tears again. I quickly wiped them away. *What is the matter with me this morning?* I asked myself. *I'm turning into a pathetic wet drip, and I'm going to have a frog face with bloodshot swollen eyes and a big red nose from crying so much.*

Outside the window, I could see Mom beginning to load up the car. Her normally glossy chestnut (highlighted) hair was scraped back into a ponytail, and she had the teeniest bit of gray coming through at her temples. *Oh, bummer*, I thought. *My fault.* Giving up her regular hairdressing appointments had been one of the sacrifices that she'd made to pay for the school. At least Dad didn't have to worry about hair. He'd lost most of his in his 30s. I'd said goodbye to him last night since he started work so early in the morning. He'd looked tired, as he often did on Sunday evenings. I was going to miss him and Mom.

"Spoiled little brat," I told myself. "Start acting your age. Opportunity of a lifetime. Blah-de-blah-de-blah."

I knew that there was no getting out of the situation. I'd tried appealing to their better natures. I'd tried begging. I'd tried rolling on the floor and moaning like a crazy girl, and clearly none of it was going to work. I knew how hard Mom and Dad had worked for me, even if I hadn't *asked* them to. Maybe I could go for a term, and then they'd realize what a mistake it was and let me come back home. *Yes, there's light at the end of the tunnel*, I decided. *Darkest hour is before dawn and all that.* With those thoughts in mind, I put on my oversize blazer, applied a bit more concealer, and brushed my hair.

Bertie was looking up at me with big, sad eyes. I felt my own eyes fill up again. *This is ridiculous*, I thought. *All I've done today is blubber, blubber, blubber.*

I bent over and put my hand out to him. He put his

paw in it in the way that I'd taught him when he was a puppy.

"Bye, boy," I said as I shook his paw and stroked his head.

"Woof," he said back.

I straightened myself up. "Right, winners never quit and quitters never win," I said to myself. "It's time to show the world that I'm not a quitter. It's walk-tall time. And I'm going to show the world that I can do it."

I took a deep breath, opened the bedroom door, tripped on the carpet, and fell flat on my face.

So much for my positive start. I hoped that it wasn't an omen.

Chapter Two

Swish school

"Are we almost there?" I asked as we passed through a small town and the road opened up into fields and trees on both sides.

Mom and Dad had already been out to Avebury to take a look around and meet the headmaster, but so far I'd only seen the brochure and didn't really know what to expect.

Mom nodded. "That's it down there," she said as we saw a huge wrought-iron gate between two brick pillars about a hundred yards down the road on our left.

I could see a grand old house with gables to the left of the gate and an immaculate yard out front. CHIRON HOUSE, said a brass plate by the front door. I peered in the windows as we passed and could see a roomful of old ladies sitting in chairs. Some were staring out the window; others appeared to be watching TV.

"But that looks like a nursing home, Mom," I said as panic rose inside me and I wondered what sort of place she was going to leave me in. If that was the staff room, the teachers were way past it.

"It *is* a nursing home," said Mom as she turned left through the gates and past the house. "The school is farther along up here. I think, in the past, Chiron House might have been a lodge for the main house."

"Maybe it's the seniors' dorm, and they've prematurely aged because they've been left without their friends and parents. I think we should turn around and go home right now."

Mom laughed. As usual, she didn't realize that I was serious.

"Or maybe it's the teachers' quarters," she said, as if we were sharing some joke. "It's more likely that the teachers have prematurely aged, not the students. Not surprising, really—it can't be easy."

"You said it!"

"I meant that it can't be easy to be a teacher," said Mom as we made our way up the long driveway lined with eucalyptus trees.

"Oooo, amazing," I said as we turned a corner and an enormous old red-brick building surrounded by acres of land came into view.

"Exactly," said Mom, looking for somewhere to park among the fleets of Range Rovers, Mercedes, and BMWs fighting for parking spaces in the courtyard at the front of the main building. "You nervous?"

"Um. Yes. No. Don't know," I replied as I gazed out the window. I didn't know what I felt. Anticipation.

Excitement. Terror.

"It is impressive, isn't it?" said Mom with a quick glance up at the house as she found a space at the end of the driveway and began to maneuver the car into it. "It looks more like a hotel than a school."

I nodded. "I wonder if they do breakfast in bed. Make mine a chocolate milk shake and fries."

Mom laughed and turned off the engine. "Ready?" she asked as she smoothed down her skirt.

I nodded again. I wanted to get out of the car as soon as possible because I couldn't help but feel that Mom's little old Ford Taurus looked out of place amid the expensive-looking cars, but no one seemed to take much notice. Car doors were opening, shutting, trunks slamming, cases being hauled up the driveway by exhausted-looking parents as girls greeted each other with shrieks and hugs. Some older girls slouched inside, looking cool and indifferent, like they couldn't wait to get rid of their parents. Others, like me, got out of their cars and looked around nervously. I don't think that I'd ever felt so small in my whole life. Although I wasn't exactly a tadpole, as I'd be going into eighth grade and the youngest students were in seventh grade, I could see that I was still among the little starter squirts, wide-eyed and anxious.

Mom took a letter out of her bag and glanced at it. "Okay. We have to look for someone in a yellow

T-shirt with 'Europa' written on it," she said and then looked around at the crowd.

"Over there," I said as I spotted a tall girl with long blond hair standing by a stone angel near the main door in the courtyard. She had a notepad and seemed to be checking off students before sending them inside. "Yellow's for my house. Europa."

"Okay. You go over and let her know that we're here," said Mom, "and I'll get your bags. You take the little one from the backseat that you can wheel."

I pulled out the wheeled suitcase and made my way over to the girl in yellow and the small group around her. She looked at her pad and then up at us.

"Hi," she said. "I'm Fleur Maclean. I'm one of the resident advisers, and I'll be showing you the ropes. There are four houses in the school: Europa, Io, Ganymede, and Callisto. All named after the four moons of Jupiter. Your house will be the same as mine, Europa. First, give me your names so that I can check them off. Then go into the main hall, down the corridor on the right, and into Room Thirty, where your housemother, Mrs. Blain, is waiting. She'll show you to your rooms."

Dutifully, we gave our names and then trooped into the main hall. I took a quick look at the other girls. There were five of them, and they looked younger than me, so they were probably new seventh-grade girls. They looked as bewildered as I felt. *At least they're all in this together*, I thought as I looked around for someone else my age who might be starting. *It won't be so bad if there's a few of us, and maybe I'll get to share a room with someone really nice. Although it won't be Jess or any of my old friends, at least I might make a new friend.*

Mom hoisted my bags after me into the main hall, and we looked around. The walls were wood paneled, with corridors leading off in all directions. An enormous staircase led up to a stunning stained glass window of a godlike figure with the sun blazing out behind him. The atmosphere was the complete opposite of my old school, which was a rundown 1970s building that smelled like sour milk and boiled cabbage. Here the air was fragrant with beeswax and flowers from the many huge arrangements on the polished tables around the hall.

"I have to go and meet my housemother," I said, pointing down one of the corridors. "I'll meet you back here in five minutes."

Mom nodded and, for a moment, looked as young as some of the new inmates.

I was determined to be grown-up about things from now on. It was my first day, and I didn't want to be pegged as a baby right from the get-go. *It is daunting, though*, I thought as I hurried to find Room 30. *So many corridors, so many rooms. I'll never find my way around. I must tell Mom that I'll need a compass for navigation and a thermos and sandwiches in case I get lost.*

I tried one door, but it was a storage closet. Then another, which looked like a coatroom. Just as I was coming out, Sara Jenkins walked past with her friends, all of whom had the same long, blond, highlighted hair.

"Hi, Sara," I said, giving her my best smile.

"Sorry, do I know you?" she asked as she looked me up and down, taking in my uniform (of course, hers fit perfectly).

"Um, not really. We live near each other. I'm starting today."

"Good for you," drawled Sara, and then she whispered something to one of her friends.

"Um. Sure you haven't got the wrong uniform on?" asked her friend from behind a curtain of long, fair hair.

"Nope, same one as you," I said. "One size fits all. I must be so petite that mine hangs off me, while yours . . . well, it fits perfectly, doesn't it?"

The girl blushed, and Sara scowled at me and was about to say something back when a blond lady with a round face and an enormous bosom came bustling forward.

"New arrival?" she asked, looking at me.

Sara's scowl disappeared and was replaced with a

sunny smile. "Yes, Mrs. Blain. We were just showing her the way."

"Good girls. In there," she said, pointing at a door.

Once inside, she checked off our names on her list and then gave us our room numbers. There were squeals of delight when Sara and her friends realized that they would be rooming together again.

"And you, Gemma . . . ?" she asked, looking at me.

"Gemma Whiting, ma'am."

"I've put you in with another new girl named Ruth Parker," she said. "You can find your way around together. Room Twenty-two on the second floor of the Europa wing. Now if you all go back to the main hall, one of the resident advisers will be there to give you your sheet of events for the rest of the day."

Ruth Parker, I thought. *I wonder what she's going to be like.* I was glad that I hadn't been put in with one of Sara's crowd—from the looks they were giving me behind Mrs. Blain's back, they had clearly decided that I was a bad smell.

Chapter Three
School mouse

"You can go now," I said to Mom after Fleur had shown us up to my room and Mom had unpacked all my stuff.

"No, no, I can stay a bit longer," said Mom as she fussed around, arranging my books on a bookcase on the right-hand side of the room.

The room wasn't bad. Pretty cheerful, in fact, for a prison cell, with rose-colored sheets and curtains and white furniture. It had a pretty view over the yard and trees at the back.

"Which bed do you want?" asked Mom, pointing at the single beds on both sides of the room.

"I'll let Ruth choose," I said. I was determined to be friends with my roommate when she arrived. It would be so cool. Being an only child, I'd never had to share my room except for sleepovers. This could be like having a sleepover every night. Maybe Ruth could be the sister that I'd never had.

After everything was unpacked, Mom was still hovering, and I was eager to start exploring.

"You can go now, Mom," I said again and pointed to the piece of paper that Fleur had given to me earlier. "I have to be shown around with the seventh graders."

Mom turned pale. "Are . . . are you sure you'll be okay? You won't be lonely?"

As I ushered her toward the door, I got the feeling that *she* was the one who was going to be feeling lonely.

"I'll be fine," I said as she looked close to tears. "Now you have to be brave, Mom. Come on. Chin up."

She smiled weakly. "It's supposed to be me saying that to you."

I smiled back at her, and together we made our way back downstairs and to the car, where she looked like she was going to start blubbering again. I was determined that I wasn't going to. I'd done my crying. A part of me couldn't help but be curious, and I was dying to look around.

Finally, Mom got into the car and drove off, and I turned back to face the rest of my first day. Mom shouldn't have worried about me being lonely. There wasn't time. As the last cars carrying parents disappeared down the driveway, the RAs went into overdrive. We were organized into groups of four and given the grand tour. The school was immense—four wings, one for each of the houses. There was an Olympic-size swimming pool and a gym in a modern annex at the back, tennis courts, a vast library, and a clinic where we were told that there were doctors, dentists, and opticians on call should we ever need any of them. Outside the kitchen of one of the wings, there was a vegetable garden, a henhouse, and a small enclosure with a couple of goats and a donkey. Each house had its own dining room and a common room with a TV and a toaster. Finally we were shown the apartment at the top of our wing, where Mrs. Blain lived, though we were told not to go up there "unless there was an emergency."

I was beginning to enjoy myself. It was like I'd been left at a sleepaway camp, and my earlier misgivings were starting to disappear. *It can only get better when I meet Ruth,* I thought. *My very own roommate to share it all with, and, like me, she won't know anyone. I can't wait.*

After the tour, the RAs handed out welcome packs with maps, schedules, sheets of information, and an invitation to meet at one o'clock in the dining room for pizza and a question-and-answer session. I raced upstairs to the second floor to see if Ruth Parker had arrived yet.

I flung open the door to see a girl lying on the bed reading a book. She was tiny. And I mean tiny—I'm not tall, at five foot two, but she looked like she was only around nine years old. *Maybe she's one of these genius-type people who are way ahead of their age,* I thought.

"Hi," I said. "You must be Ruth. I was wondering where you were."

The girl glanced up nervously, and I couldn't help but think that she looked like a startled mouse. She even had hair the color of a mouse, light brown and tied back in a severe braid.

"Hello," she said and then went back to her book.

"I'm Gemma. Gemma Whiting. I'm going to be sharing a room with you."

"Oh," said Ruth with another quick glance up. "Okay. I've put my things away. I hope that's all right."

"Course," I said. "It's your room, too. Have you had a look around?"

Ruth shook her head. "Not really."

"Well, there are lots of RAs showing people around and pizza in the dining room if you're hungry and . . ."

"No, thanks," said Ruth.

"Are you sad to leave home?" I asked.

No answer, just a tiny shrug of one of her tiny shoulders. "My parents have gone overseas, so I don't have a home, really. They've rented it out while they work out their contract over there."

Oh, this is going to be fun, I thought. *Not*. But I couldn't help feeling sorry for her; at least my parents were only a couple of hours away.

"What are you reading?"

"Philip Pullman," she said.

"Is it good?"

Another shrug and a brief nod. *Well, she's lively*, I

23

thought. *But maybe she wants to be left alone. Maybe she's sad about her parents leaving and needs some quiet time.*

I waited for a few moments in the hope that she might say something else, but she seemed deeply engrossed in her book.

"Okay," I said. "I'm going down for some food. I'll be back later."

Another shrug. So I left.

I made my way down the stairs and into the dining room, where a crowd of girls were digging into lunch. I wished that Ruth had come down with me so that I had someone to talk to, because, besides the seventh graders, all of the other girls already knew each other.

I went to the buffet table and helped myself to some pizza and then looked for somewhere to sit. There was one space at a table where Sara Jenkins and her friends were sitting. Sara saw me eye the spare chair, and she quickly put her bag on it. I got the message—not wanted there. I made my way over to the window and pretended to be fascinated by the view. *I hope Ruth livens up a bit*, I thought as I stared intently at a rosebush and tried not to look too self-conscious. *I don't like this awkward feeling of not knowing anyone.*

The dining room looked out onto the front, and in the distance I could see a motorcycle coming up the driveway. Then I heard someone say, "Oh, here's

Hermie," and a group of older girls rushed out. I took a closer look to see who was on the bike. Whoever he was, he was tearing down the driveway at full speed. For lack of anything better to do or anyone to talk to, I decided to go out and join the group of girls who were already waiting in the courtyard.

"Who's Hermie?" I asked a girl with short dark hair who'd obviously had the same idea.

"Don't know," she said as we reached the front, "but his bike looks cool."

As Hermie approached and saw the gathering crowd, he stood up on the seat and did a handstand on the handlebars. The crowd gasped in admiration. I caught my breath since I thought he was going to fall off any minute—what he was doing looked really precarious. He didn't stay up long, though, and swung back down into the seat, revved up, reared the front wheel up into the air, and screeched to a stop outside the main door. There he turned off his bike, took off his helmet, ran his fingers through his glossy shoulder-length dark hair, shook out his hair some more, and gave his admirers a huge smile. All of the older girls, including Fleur, turned red and smiled coyly back at him. He was clearly a hit with the juniors and seniors.

I laughed. It was like watching a shampoo commercial where some impossibly gorgeous model flicks perfect hair this way and that way for the camera. Like—flickety-flick. *Look at me. I'm so beautiful.* I had to admit that he *was* good-looking, though, like one of those statues of a Greek god. I was just trying to figure out how old he was—maybe 19, maybe in his 20s—when an elderly man with white hair and a beard came rushing out the front door. He looked furious.

"Oops," said a girl behind me. "Here comes trouble."

"Who's that?" I asked.

"Headmaster," said the girl. "Dr. Cronus. Stay out of his way if you can. He can be a real slave driver if you get him in the wrong mood."

"And what sort of insane display do you call that?" yelled Dr. Cronus. "This is a school, for heaven's sake, not a circus."

Hermie grinned. "Hi, Grandpa," he said. "Delivery for one of the girls."

Dr. Cronus then turned to the crowd of girls. "And what are you all staring at?"

I looked at the floor and shuffled around, trying to pretend that I wasn't really there. I didn't want to get in trouble on my first day.

Dr. Cronus sighed. "For the sake of the new girls, I suppose I'd better introduce you," he said to Hermie. "Girls, gather around. This is Hermie. He's our messenger. If any of you has mail to send, he'll take it, and he will also bring our mail and packages from outside to us. All mail can be left in the main hall in the marked box."

One of the girls giggled, and Dr. Cronus gave her a stern look.

"And what's so funny about that?" he asked.

"Um . . . nothing," said the girl. "Nothing at all."

Hermie took off his leather jacket to reveal a black sleeveless T-shirt with the words "Mercury Communications" on it and toned, tanned arms. I also noticed that he had some stars tattooed on his right arm and four star-shaped earrings in his left ear. He didn't look like the grandson of Dr. Cronus at all, as the headmaster looked like he belonged to another, ancient age. Hermie was really hot and definitely of this century. He gave a little bow, and another girl giggled and then quickly stifled it when she saw Dr. Cronus look at her.

"Only one package today," said Hermie, producing a box from the back of his bike. "Ta-DAH! For the one and only Gemma Whiting."

I felt myself turn red as everyone looked around to see who Gemma Whiting was. I put up my hand and made my way forward.

Hermie looked right into my eyes before handing me the package. I felt myself turn even redder, even though his expression was kind. "Ah. So it's *you*!" he said. "Your lucky day, hon."

I took the package from him. "Um . . . thank you very much."

By now, even more girls had come out, including Sara and her friends. Everyone was looking at me and my package.

"Have a good day," said Hermie as he tied his jacket around his waist, jumped back on his bike, put his helmet back on, and revved up his engine. He gave his grandfather a cheery wave and then took off. As he passed Sara and her friends, he spun his front wheel so that it made gravel from the driveway fly up and hit their legs. Sara leaped back, and as Hermie rode past me I swear that he winked at me.

"Okay. Enough of this," said Dr. Cronus. "Settle down now. Back inside." And he disappeared through the front door.

"What is it?" asked the dark-haired girl as a crowd now gathered around me. "What have you been sent?"

"Don't know," I said as I tore open the package. All eyes were on me once again, and I felt a mixture of curiosity and embarrassment at being the center of so much attention.

Inside was a turquoise glittery cell phone wrapped in bubble wrap, a silver necklace, and a card. The phone was state-of-the-art designer cool, and the necklace was delicate and exquisite. Both items looked like they had cost megabucks, and I wondered who on earth could have sent me such gorgeous things. *There must be a mistake*, I thought.

"What's on the chain?" asked one of the girls, looking closely at the necklace.

"Looks like a zodiac symbol," said Fleur. "Yes. It's the twins. For Gemini. Is that your sign, Gemma?"

I nodded. Maybe it wasn't a mistake.

"Same as me," said Fleur. "I'm a Gemini, too, so that's how I knew."

"And *cool* phone," said one of her friends.

"What does the card say?" asked Sara, who had suddenly decided to take an interest.

"Don't know," I said as I read the card. I was hoping that it would tell me who the gifts were from, but there was no message on it. In fact, it looked like a business card with an address on one side, and on the other side, in small print, there were a few facts about Geminis:

"Gemini: an air sign; rules the arms, chest, and lungs; colors are yellow and silver; lucky day: Wednesday; birthstone: emerald/agate; keywords: *lively, communicative, adaptable, multifaceted, sharp-witted, mentally active, independent*; ruled by Mercury."

"Don't know much, do you?" scoffed Sara, and she reached out and grabbed the phone. "Neat phone, though." She flicked it open. "I think it's one of those video camera phones." She pressed a few buttons, but the phone appeared to be dead. I wanted her to give it back to me—it had been sent to me, not her—but she didn't seem in any hurry to hand it over.

One of her friends snatched the card and began to read it out loud. "It's a website address," she said as she turned it over and read the other side as well. "For some zodiac thing. Huh. Are you a New Age nut then, Gemma—into astrology?"

I took the card back from her. "No," I said. I was as baffled as everyone else was by the mysterious gifts. *Who could possibly have sent them?* I wondered. *No way could my mom or dad or my friends have afforded things like that.*

In the meantime, Sara was roughly pressing all the buttons on the phone, trying to make it work. Suddenly an image appeared on the screen. It looked like a green blobby monster, and Sara leaped back, but not before the face on the screen was joined by the words "Get OFF me, Miss Snot Face."

A couple of girls who were close enough to read the message burst out laughing, and Sara dropped the phone like it was a hot potato.

"I don't like it," she said. "It's weird." She linked arms with her friends and sneered at me. "And *you're* weird. You can keep your stupid phone. And your necklace. It's probably a cheap giveaway for some astrology site or something, anyway."

It's not a cheap giveaway, I thought as I picked up the

phone from the ground to see that a new face had appeared on the screen. It was an image of Hermie smiling and giving me the thumbs-up. *Wow,* I thought. *It's one of those camera phones. I've always wanted one of those, but . . . where did the green thing disappear to?* Sara was right. The whole thing *was* weird, but I wasn't going to give her the satisfaction of seeing that I was fazed by it. I glanced up to see that some of the older girls were looking suspiciously at me.

"So, who sent you the phone?" asked Fleur.

"Not sure," I replied as I clicked it shut. "Um. Probably my dad or someone."

"So did Hermie leave you his number?" asked Fleur.

"*Me?* No. No way," I said as I glanced down at the card. The girls clearly had the hots for Hermie and didn't like the thought of any competition. "I think Sara was right. The card is probably some sort of a promotion for an astrology site. Probably put in the bag when whoever bought my presents got them. You know how it goes. Store assistants are always putting all sorts of stuff in bags with your purchases to advertise stuff. Pizzas. Free cell phones. Vacations in the Caribbean. Zodiac stuff. Not my thing."

I was aware that I was rambling and ought to shut up. "And . . . anyway, even if Hermie had left me his number, which he hasn't, I'm not into boys or anything. Yeah. I think I might as well toss the card."

"Around the back, outside the kitchen," drawled one of Fleur's friends as she flicked her hair off her face and then slouched back inside.

Phew, I think I handled that okay, I thought as I made my way around the back to get rid of the card. It was going to be hard enough with Sara and her gang treating me like a reject. The last thing I needed was the older girls turning against me as well.

Chapter Four

Party time

"Winners never quit and quitters never win," I said to Ruth, who was at her desk with her head stuck in a book, as usual. We'd just had dinner and were supposed to be doing our homework, but I had other plans. I put away my books and stuck my dad's card back up on the bulletin board above my desk in our room.

It was our third day, and besides Ruth, I still hadn't made any new friends. We were the only new girls in our grade, and as I'd foreseen, the groups of friends in our class were already well established. It was hard getting in with anyone. Not that anyone—besides Sara and Co.—was unfriendly, but they just didn't need new friends. So it was me and Ruth. Ruth and I. Not that I could call Ruth a friend. She was as silent as a shadow. She never spoke to anyone and only answered if a teacher asked her a question. The sleepaway camp atmosphere hadn't lasted long, and we'd been put into our classes the day after orientation. In all of them, Ruth acted as though she wanted to be invisible. She attended them, did what was asked of her, and then got back onto her bed with one of her books as soon as possible. I wanted more. I'd seen the groups of girls in the dining room or in the common room, gossiping, catching up, laughing the way I used to with Jess and my other friends. I wasn't about to give in. *I've always had friends. I'm a Gemini, and Geminis LIKE people, like being with people,* I thought. *I want to be in and out of someone's room, chatting, swapping stories, telling jokes, finding out what's happening. I'm not about to become a loner now.*

"I think we should have a midnight feast," I said, "only not at midnight because that's too late. At ten. A ten o'clock feast. You know that saying—if you want a friend, be a friend? That's what I'm going to be. Everybody's friend. Starting tonight. I've done some invitations on my pink notepaper asking everyone to come here, and I'm going to go and put them under everyone's door while people are in their rooms doing their homework. It's bound to work. There's not much on TV tonight, so who could resist? I've got chips and M&Ms, a whole bunch of goodies that Mom left me."

Ruth looked up, and I could see panic in her eyes.

"Is that okay with you?" I asked.

"But . . . but it's lights out at ten."

I rolled my eyes. "I know. That's the point. Having a feast when you're supposed to be tucked in bed."

"But it's against the rules. We'll . . . you'll get in trouble."

"No one will know. It'll be fine, but is it okay with you? I mean, this is your room, too, and . . . well . . . you need to make friends, too."

Ruth shook her head. "Me? No. I'd rather not. But then I don't want to ruin it for you. I'll . . . I'll go to the library."

"Oh, *please* don't do that, Ruth. Anyway, it will be closed. You won't have to do much. I'll do all the talking. I just think that I . . . we . . . need to put out the hand of friendship. If you disappear, people will think that you're stuck-up or that you don't like anyone or something."

"I'll go and take a shower then. A very long shower," said Ruth, and then she sighed. "I just want to be left alone."

I sighed. "I've gathered that."

Ruth sighed again. "Sorry."

I sighed again, and then I laughed. "Look, we can't spend the whole year with both of us sighing every minute . . ."

But Ruth wasn't listening anymore. She was gathering together her shower stuff for later.

"Okay," I said. "I won't push you. I want *us* to get along at least. You go and take a shower if you want. And take some of my coconut-and-vanilla body wash. It smells amazing."

Ruth gave me half a smile. "Thanks," she said as I

went back to my invitations and sprinkled a little glitter inside each of the envelopes. When they were done, I delivered them to all of the rooms on our floor and even to Sara Jenkins and her friends Mercedes, Tasha, and Lois, as I didn't want to leave anyone out. It would be great. Everyone would be able to come— what else were they going to be doing? They'd be so pleased to have been invited, and mine would be the very first party of the school year.

When I'd delivered the last invitation, I went back to my room and got out all the supplies: soda and chips and chocolate-chip cookies. At five minutes to ten, Ruth got up to go take her shower, but before she left, she opened the drawer in her night table and got out a huge bar of milk chocolate.

"Here. This is for your ten o'clock feast," she said, and then she scurried out before I could persuade her to stay. I broke up the chocolate into pieces and put it on a plate next to the other goodies. Then I waited.

And waited.

And waited.

I got out my new cell phone for the tenth time since I'd received it to see if whoever had sent it had left a message or, even better, thought to give me some free talk time so that I could call my old friends, but there was nothing. Not the strange face and voice that was rude to Sara. Not the image of Hermie. Neither instructions, nor a voice mail, nor a text message. *What's the point of it?* I asked myself as I put it back in the drawer.

Five past ten.

Ten past ten.

Quarter past.

Nobody.

I opened the door to check that the number "22" hadn't fallen off by mistake, but, no, it was still there.

Twenty past ten. Still no one. Where was everyone?

I opened the door to see if anyone was coming, but the corridor was empty. I went down to the common room to see if maybe everyone was watching TV, but there were only two older girls in there—Fleur and her friend Sophie.

Maybe they're all asleep, I thought, but as I made my way back up to my floor, I could hear the sounds of laughter down at the opposite end of the corridor to where my room was. I followed the noise.

It was coming from Sara and Mercedes' room, and inside I could hear Sara's voice and then Lois's. *They must be having their own ten o'clock feast*, I thought. Already they'd established themselves as the cool girls of our class, and I hadn't really expected them to come to my room. They would see it as beneath them to hang out with a new girl who hadn't proved herself to be as popular as they were. Sometimes I think there must be an unspoken law that goes: "If thou art one of the prettiest girls in class, thou shalt not hang out with less pretty classmates with great big zits on their foreheads." But then I heard what sounded like Imogen's voice, and she's not friends with them. She's in the room next to mine with Rose Watson. I pressed my ear to the door. There was definitely a whole crowd of people in there, and it sounded like they were having a really good time.

Suddenly the door opened, and Rose came flying out. "Ooomf," she said as she crashed into me. "Oh, Gemma. Sorry. Didn't see you there."

Now I could see into the room, and everyone from my floor was there. Everyone except Ruth and me.

"Oh," said Mercedes, getting up off the bed. "Gemma."

I wanted the ground to open up and swallow me. "Yes. Sorry. Um . . ."

Tasha got up and stood next to Mercedes. "Hi, Gemma. Um, yes. We didn't invite you because . . . because . . ."

Mercedes took over. "Because we knew that you were having your own party . . ."

"That's what gave us the idea, in fact," added Lois with a fake smile.

"Yes . . ." Tasha stuttered, "and that's why we didn't invite you, because, um . . ."

I could see that she was desperately trying to think up some excuse, but it wasn't coming to her very fast. However, unlike Sara and Mercedes, she looked embarrassed. I thought that she might be nicer than her friends, because sometimes I'd caught her looking at me, and once she even smiled.

"We thought you were babysitting your mouse," said Sara from the bed, where she was curled up like a cat.

Everyone laughed. In one way I couldn't blame them, because I'd thought the same thing on my first day. Ruth did resemble a mouse. A sweet mouse, but a mouse all the same.

"Doesn't matter," I said as I began to stumble back down the corridor. "Um. Just thought I heard something. Never mind."

Mercedes shut the door, and for a moment there was silence. Then I heard them all burst out laughing at the same time.

I crept back into my room and closed the door. All the food looked so pathetic, and Ruth's chocolate was beginning to melt. I was so hurt that it felt like someone had kicked me in the stomach, so I got on my bed and curled up against the wall. I wished that I had Bertie there with me to make me feel better. He'd never reject me or have a doggy feast with his friends without inviting me. Dogs aren't like that. They're loyal. Girls can be so mean. There'd been a gang of them at my last school, but I'd never been on the receiving end of their nastiness. Lucy, Chloe, Ellie, Jess, Charlotte, and I looked out for each other. For the first time, I wondered if there had been girls like Ruth—and now me—at my last school. I'd been so busy having a great time with all my friends that I'd never noticed or thought to look.

I really wanted to talk to Jess, but it was almost 11:00 P.M. Her mom would kill me. And talking to her might only make me feel worse. She'd called my room on Monday night from Ellie's house. All the gang was there, and they'd passed the phone around and said how much they were missing me. Didn't sound like it. It sounded like they were having a whale of a time. Last night, I'd called them one by one, and I'd soon used up half the minutes on my phone card as they filled me in on the gossip from their school. I hadn't said too much because I didn't want to admit that in my first week of school I was the outsider and I was having a miserable time.

I thought about calling Mom. She'd be home from teaching her classes at the night school, but I decided against it. I didn't want to upset her, and she'd probably think I was a baby for feeling like this in the first week. *Only one thing to do*, I thought, as the plate of chocolate stared up at me with a dark, velvety smile.

I'd eaten half the bar when there was a timid knock on the door. I sat up and smoothed my hair. Maybe someone had realized how cruel they'd been to leave me out and had come to apologize.

"Come in," I called.

The door opened a fraction of an inch, and Ruth popped her head around.

"Is it okay to come back in yet?" she asked.

"Oh, yes," I said, turning back to the wall.

"Has everyone left?" she asked as she crept in.

"No one even showed up."

"Oh."

"Yes. Oh."

I heard Ruth pad over to her side of the room and the bed creak as she got onto it. I glanced over my shoulder to see that she had taken up the same position that I'd been in a moment earlier. So there we were, rejects, both lying on our beds with our faces to the wall.

I turned and lay on my back and looked at the ceiling. I felt like I was going to burst. "Ruth, have you always been so quiet?"

"Um. Suppose."

"But why? Don't you ever want to talk to someone? Say how you're feeling? Find out what other people are feeling?"

"No."

More silence as I continued staring at the ceiling. Ruth had started reading. *Ah, well, never mind*, I thought as I got my Harry Potter book out of my night table. Harry had had a hard time with Draco Malfoy when he first went to his boarding school. Maybe I could find some good advice on how to handle mean girls in the book. *Probably helps if you're a wizard like Harry, though*, I thought as I read a few pages. Now *that* would have been something—if instead of being given a useless phone, I'd been given a magic wand. I could have turned Sara, Mercedes, Lois, and Tasha into toads or monkeys or puddles of green slime or made them sprout hair from their foreheads and grow boils on their butts and make their hair drop out and grow back frizzy and bright orange. For a while, I lay on the bed having a most enjoyable fantasy of what I could do if I had magical powers, but as the minutes ticked on, my imagination began to run dry, and I couldn't deny the fact that I wasn't at a school with Harry Potter, a boy who had great adventures. I was at a school with Ruth Parker, a girl who didn't want to leave her room if she could help it. I wasn't a witch. I was me. Plain, ordinary me. Miles from home. On a bed, at a boarding school, with no friends. It stank.

"Ruth?"

"Yes."

"Have you ever had any friends?"

Ruth looked over at me with her big, sad eyes and nodded. "One. Naomi. She went to live in Australia."

"And after that?"

"Not really. My family was always moving around, so I was always the new girl. I stopped trying after a while."

"But why? Everyone needs friends. It makes life so much better."

Ruth shook her head. "I . . . I got picked on after Naomi left. It's best just to be quiet. The best way to survive is not to bother anyone. You don't get hurt that way. If you hadn't tried to have that midnight—I mean, ten o'clock—feast, you wouldn't have gotten hurt, and now look, you're upset."

It was the most I'd heard her say since she'd arrived. And she was right. So much for my "if you want a friend, be a friend" speech. No one wanted to know me. No one had come to check that I was okay and that I wasn't upset. I settled back down to my book. Maybe I'd become a bookworm. Get ahead with all of my homework. And I could always catch up with my friends during break. I got up to calculate the days left until the next school break. It was a long time. Day after day with no friends. Then seven days at break with friends. It didn't sound like much fun.

I tried reading again but couldn't concentrate. I

didn't want to spend the rest of my life without any friends.

"No. I'm *not* giving in," I said to the ceiling. I glanced over at Ruth to see if she was going to comment, but she'd put on her headphones and hadn't heard me. *Huh*, I thought, *why did I get landed with you? It's not fair. You don't want any friends, but I do. And if I'd gotten another roommate, it might have been okay. It's so, so, so not fair. I'm in danger of becoming like you if I don't watch out, a timid little thing who's scared to try anything, and that's not me. Maybe it's just a bad patch. Darkest hour just before dawn and all that. I wish someone could tell me that it's going to get better.*

"It's your lucky day," that stupid messenger boy had told me on Monday. *Just shows what he knew*, I thought. *So why did he give the phone to me? Maybe there is something I missed. Some button I haven't pressed.* I got off the bed and got the phone out of the drawer. I turned it on and was about to try pressing some buttons when it beeped that there was a message for me. It was so unexpected that I almost jumped out of my skin. I threw it across the bed in case it did anything strange and then sat and watched it for a while. It didn't appear to be doing anything too odd, just lying there innocently, so I picked it up and read the message.

"Go to your computer and visit the site," it said.

I scrolled down for the rest of the message.

There was no rest of the message.

What site? I thought. Then I remembered the card

44

that Hermit or Hermie or whatever he was called had left me. It was for an astrology website. Why had I thrown it away? Because I was trying to worm my way in with the older girls by showing them that I wasn't into boys, that's why. But maybe this Hermie had been trying to tell me something. Maybe the stars were in a bad place for me, but the phase would pass.

I quickly grabbed my jacket, let myself out of our room, and crept downstairs. Everywhere was quiet, and the main lights were turned off. There was just a glow from the nightlight down in the hall. *I wish I'd brought a flashlight*, I thought as I tiptoed along to the dining room and then into the kitchen, praying that the back door was open. Boris, the school cat, was asleep on one of the windowsills at the back of the kitchen. He lazily opened one eye and then fell back asleep.

"Good cat, good Boris," I said as I tried the door.

It was locked, with two enormous bolts, one at the top and one at the bottom. I pulled back the bottom one and then pulled over a chair to reach the top one. Two minutes later, I was outside.

The moment I stepped outside, a security light came on and flooded the area. I darted behind a Dumpster, where I giggled to myself. Not because it was funny, but because I was feeling nervous. Although I'd joked about the school being a prison, this was like in the movies when a prisoner tries to

45

escape. *Any minute now*, I thought, *a siren's going to wail, and the teachers are going to appear at the windows with guns.* I glanced up, but the windows were dark. It was going to be okay.

There were three enormous Dumpsters to the right of the kitchen door. *Now which one did I throw the card into?* I asked myself. *And why am I even doing this? It's crazy. Why don't I just text Hermie back and say that I lost the card? No, better not*, I decided. He might think that I was ignoring him, and after earlier this evening, I knew only too well how horrible that felt.

Okay, winners never quit, I thought as I hoisted myself up onto a pile of boxes and climbed into the first Dumpster. *Thank God those security lights are on, or I wouldn't be able to see a thing.*

I spent the next five minutes sifting through trash bags full of vegetable peelings, pieces of paper, and rotting fruit. It smelled *disgusting.* Of decaying meat and rotten eggs mixed with some moldy cheese. Not my favorite odor.

And then I saw it. The card was stuck to the side of the Dumpster at the top on the right. I pulled it off and began to climb out.

Suddenly, a window opened on the first floor, and a face peered out. It was Sara, and she was soon joined by Mercedes.

"Is someone out there?" called Mercedes.

Sara looked over the area as I ducked down, but too late. She'd seen me. I heard her snort back laughter.

"It's Gemma Whiting! There. In the trash."

Mercedes looked over to where she'd pointed and burst out laughing, too. "Aw, Gemma. Didn't have enough dinner, baby? Feeling a bit hungry-wungry?"

"No. Someone put her out with the trash," Sara said with a snicker.

"Neither, actually," I said as I climbed out as gracefully as I could, which was hard, seeing as I had to hoist my leg up and then haul myself over the side. "Actually, I lost something."

Then I pulled myself up tall and tried my best to look as dignified as possible. A difficult feat with a banana peel on my head and a lettuce leaf stuck to my left ear.

Chapter Five

Zodiac Girl

Ruth was asleep by the time I got back to our room. I waited until the next morning when she'd gone to the bathroom, and then I quickly opened my laptop. I logged onto the Internet and typed in the astrology site address.

Soft space-age music began to play as a night sky full of stars and planets appeared on the screen. As the site downloaded, a pale blue form appeared, asking for my name, birthday, and place of birth. I dutifully typed them in and pressed the "submit" button.

A second later, the screen burst into life, and if no one was awake on our floor, they would have been then as a fanfare of trumpets blasted out of the computer and the screen lit up with flashing lights and bursts of fireworks.

"Wow!" I said as I leaped back into my chair. "What the . . . ?"

"Congratulations, Gemma Gemini," flashed a message across the sky, "YOU are this month's ZODIAC GIRL." And the fanfare grew louder, tan-tan-na-da-DA-DA-DA-DA-DA.

The form on the screen swirled around a bit and then disappeared, and what looked like some sort of map with lines all over it took its place. "Your personal birth chart," it said underneath. After that there were pages of writing. Sun in Gemini, rising sign is Aries, Moon in Cancer, Mars in Aries, Venus in Cancer, Uranus in Capricorn, and on it went, saying that this planet was here, that planet was there. None of it made any sense to me, except that I was a Gemini. And I already knew that, as my birthday is May 26.

So what? I thought as I scanned the pages. *Why does Hermie want me to know all of this, unless he's some kind of astrology nut?* I was just about to shut the computer down when a blurry message flashed onto the right of the screen.

"Hey, Gemma. Gemini. Zodiac Girl. Ruled by Mercury. Ask for help. You'll get it."

And that was it.

The screen went back to playing its spacey music again. *So, big deal. I'm a Gemini with Aries rising or whatever. Is that it?* I felt disappointed. I don't know what I'd been hoping for, but this certainly wasn't it. There weren't any words of wisdom to see me through, and the site certainly wasn't going to help me make new friends by advising me on what to do or say. Like, "Hi there. I know you might have thought that I was crazy at first and a bit pimply at the moment, but hey, wait a minute, I'm a Zodiac Girl!" And everyone would fall at my feet. Pfff. The site was a letdown. But it *had* said to ask for help and I'd get it. *Ask whom for help?* I wondered.

I went back to the cell phone to see if maybe I'd missed something and there was a clue as to what I should do next.

There was nothing in the in box except an image of Hermie looking very pleased with himself. *Ah, well,* I thought. *Never mind.* It was still a cool phone, so maybe I'd be able to use it instead of my boring old one. If nothing else, I could use it to call my friends. I pressed the button for the address book and found that someone had already got there before me.

Hermie.

Hermie again, I thought. *What nerve! Who does he think he is, leaving his number? What a bighead. He may have half the upper class swooning over him, but not me. I bet his plan is to give a phone to all of the new inmates over the next few weeks. He probably got them free with his job at Mercury Communications, and giving them away is his way of getting everyone's attention. Well, not me, pal.*

I decided to call and tell him so.

"Hey, Zodiac Girl," he said when I got through a moment later.

"Yeah. It's me. Gemma Gemini. Who's not going to be part of your fan club just because you gave me a cell phone with a photo of you looking particularly nauseating. I'm sorry, but you're not my type. Waaay too old. And I don't go for the motorcycle thing." Then I thought that I might have hurt his feelings, as I had read in one of Chloe's magazines once that it's hard for boys, having to take rejection. "Look, sorry, but I don't like you, and anyway, I'm only in eighth grade. No hard feelings."

Hermie seemed to be having a fit of laughter at the other end. "Sure, no hard feelings," he said and chuckled. "But did you look at the site closely?"

"Yeah—it said that I get help for a month. And that was it."

"Look again," said Hermie. "Come on, Gemma Gemini. Chill out a bit. Give it a try. You've got nothing to lose. Go back to the site. I think you'll find something you might like there. Your birth chart is well aspected by Venus this week."

"Aspected?"

"It means where your personal planets are in relation to each other."

And then he hung up.

As instructed, I went back to the site. At first, nothing happened. Then the spacey music started to play again, and blurry words appeared. I strained to read them. Something about Pluto being square to Mercury and Jupiter making me highly persuasive. Renewed energy and, for one month, the chance to make my mark and find my calling and then a bunch of stuff about planets being square and sextile. It made no sense to me until a candy-pink certificate lined with silver appeared at the top left of the screen. A line at the bottom of it flashed in enormous writing, "PRINT ME OUT." At least I could see *that* clearly.

I'd just printed it out and was reading it when Ruth came back in.

"Oh, NO!" I cried. "I don't believe it!"

"What? What's happened?" she asked.

I threw the certificate on the floor. "That pug-faced diaper bucket of a messenger, Hermie. He just sent me a certificate for a makeover. A *makeover*! Can you believe it?" I felt mortified. How could I have been so stupid? To think that I'd imagined that he liked me. Of course he didn't. He'd singled me out in a glance as the new girl who was most in need of a makeover! What *nerve*!

"So what's wrong with that?" asked Ruth.

"Doh. That's why he thought I needed help. He must have thought I was *so* ugly that I need to see a beautician. He must have seen my zit. And my hair. And my uniform."

Ruth picked up the certificate and smoothed it out.

"A gift certificate for Pentangle beauty salon . . . and oh, wow, Gemma, it says that the budget is unlimited. 'Whatever it takes, whatever the cost, whatever the recipient wants or needs.'"

"Pfft," I interrupted. "I bet you one of his girlfriends runs the salon and got him to give out these certificates to get her business."

"Says here that it's for two," continued Ruth as she read the certificate. "For this Saturday. And that you have to get your mom's permission. And, look, it says there's a class at the salon on Thursday night on how to find your inner goddess. That's tonight."

"My inner goddess? Yeah, right," I said as I took it from Ruth and pinned it on my bulletin board. "I won't ask Mom's permission. She can use it when she comes out this way to visit. No point in it going to waste, but I'm beyond help in the makeover department. And as for my inner goddess, I think she died."

I looked over at Ruth hopefully, but she didn't realize that this was her cue to say, *Oh, no, Gemma, you look fabulous.* Jess always did if I moaned on about my looks, and I always did if Jess was having a horrible-hair day. It was one of those unspoken rules between friends. Ruth just shrugged and looked straight at my zit.

"I think it may be going down a little," she said and then looked at my chin. "But you might be getting another one . . ."

I turned back to the mirror. She was right. Another lurker was lurking lurkily under the skin. It must have been all the chocolate I ate last night. *Huh, serves you right, you stupid thing,* I thought as I reached for my phone. I was going to tell that Hermie exactly what I thought.

"Well, hi there again, Zodiac Girl," he said when he picked up.

"A gift certificate for a makeover. What nerve! You must think I'm *so* ugly."

"Hey, no way, Gemma Gemini. I told you, your Venus is in a good place. That means she's shining some light on you this week."

"So what? What's Venus? A planet. What can that do?"

"Yeah, Venus is a planet—the planet of beauty and harmony. And it's well aspected in your chart, kiddo. I'm trying to help here, not insult you. And don't take this the wrong way, but you're pretty cute for an eighth grader."

For a moment, I was lost for words. That was the nicest thing that anyone had said to me all week. All month. All year. People used to say it all the time when I was a baby and in elementary school, and even in seventh grade I could make myself look halfway decent with a little bit of effort. But, lately, it all seemed to have gone wrong. It felt like I'd got the wrong head on the wrong body, and my hair had taken on a life of its own.

"Oh. Thanks," I stuttered. "Um. Okay. And I'm sorry if I made out like you were only giving out phones to add to your fan club."

"Not me, hon. You're the only one who got a phone. Only one Zodiac Girl at a time. And I'm not some slimeball who's out to pick up girls, you know—I'm your guardian for the month."

"My what?"

"Guardian. Every Zodiac Girl gets a guardian according to their sign."

"But why me?"

"You're a Gemini. Gemini is ruled by Mercury, so that's me."

I remembered his T-shirt. Mercury Communications. "But why? How? I mean, why only one Zodiac Girl and why is it me?"

"Everyone always asks that! It's you because the stars say it's you. They've lined up in a special way, which, to put it simply, means that you've got a tough time coming up, and the planets are going to help you through it."

"How?"

"You'll find out. Trust me. Just go with the flow. And read the site carefully the next time. You may find it useful."

When he'd hung up, I did go back to the site, and there, sure enough, it said that Gemini was ruled by the planet Mercury, and, as a Zodiac Girl, I was entitled to the aid of my personal guardian. Hermie. I felt mystified. Guardian? Ruling planet? Aspects of Venus? What was it all about? And what did Hermie have to do with any of it? Okay, so he worked for a place called Mercury Communications, but he was just a motorcycle messenger, wasn't he?

When I got down to breakfast, there seemed to be a buzz of excitement in the dining room.

"What's going on?" I asked Rose Watson, who was helping herself to toast and peanut butter from the buffet table.

She nodded her head toward the hall. "End-of-term show," she said. "There's a notice about it in the main hall. For seventh, eighth, and ninth graders."

"Really?"

Rose nodded again. "Auditions will be on Friday afternoon. Proceeds from the show are to go toward building a new science lab. Apparently, if you don't want to be in the show, you can take part in some kind of social-work outreach program."

No contest, I thought. I knew which one I wanted to take part in. Being in a show is one sure way to get friendly with people.

"What's the show going to be?"

"*Bugsy Malone*," said Rose as she moved off to join her friends Grace and Imogen.

Bugsy Malone! I thought. *Very cool.* We'd done it at my old school, and I'd played Blousey, Bugsy's girlfriend. This was heaven-sent. Maybe this was my Venus or whatever being well aspected, the stars lining up to help me like Hermie had said. If that really *was* the case, maybe I could even get the part I'd really wanted back at my old school. Tallulah. Jodie Foster had played her in the movie version, and it was the best role ever. I'd learned all of her songs by heart in case the girl playing her part got the flu or something on the night of the performance. I used to drive Mom and Dad crazy singing all of her numbers morning, noon, and night and sometimes even in my sleep, according to Mom. Tallulah was so cool, like a teen goddess. If I could get her part now, I'd be really popular. Whoever played Tallulah always was. It went hand in hand with the part.

I could hardly eat my breakfast because I felt so excited and went straight to the bulletin board afterward to sign up for the auditions. To my dismay, there were already four names down for the part of Tallulah. Lois, Sara, Mercedes, and Tasha.

Never mind, I thought, *I can audition for both parts, Tallulah and Blousey.* I glanced down to see if anyone was down for Blousey yet. The same names were there. Lois, Sara, Mercedes, and Tasha.

If you can't beat 'em, join 'em, I thought as I got out my pen and added my name to the bottom of the list.

Chapter Six

Inner goddesses

As the day went on, the "how to find your inner goddess" class and makeover began to appeal more and more. Maybe it wasn't such a bad idea. And the message on the site had said that I had one month to find my calling. *Surely it meant the part in* Bugsy. *It's fated, I thought, written in the stars—and isn't that what astrology is all about?*

At lunchtime, I called Mom.

"Gemma, is everything all right?" she asked. "Where are you? You sound like you're in a tunnel."

"I'm at school, of course. In the coatroom."

"So why are you calling now? Is something wrong?"

"No. It's lunch break. Everything's fine. It's just that I've been given a gift certificate for a beauty salon called Pentangle in town, and it says I have to get your permission to use it."

"What certificate? What are you talking about?"

"Um. Long story. On Saturdays we're allowed to go into town for a few hours. Our housemother comes with us and brings us back, so she won't be far away, and I've checked out the salon and tonight there's a workshop on goddesses . . ."

"Oh, Gemma, I'm not sure."

"I won't be by myself. My roommate will be coming with me. The certificate is for two people. So, please can I go?"

"Well, I'll check with Mrs. Blain, and then I'll get back to you. But how's school?"

"Great, and I'm up for the part of Tallulah in the school play, which is even more of a reason that I need to go to the beauty salon."

"So you're settling in all right?"

"Yep. Fine," I said. I wasn't about to tell her that my first four days had been a disaster, the part of Tallulah wasn't actually mine yet, and that I had the school mouse as a roommate. She didn't need details, and in any case, all that was about to change. All I had to do was persuade Ruth.

I found her later in the afternoon in her usual spot on her bed.

"Me? No," Ruth said and got out her book and then put on her headphones.

I went and sat cross-legged on the end of her bed until she finally had to register that I wasn't going to give up on her. Begrudgingly, she took off her headphones.

"What?" she asked.

"Trying to be invisible isn't the answer, Ruth. What we need is to change. We both need a makeover. To make the most of ourselves."

"Ah. The zodiac gift certificate."

"Yeah. My mom spoke to Mrs. Blain this afternoon, and they're okay with the gift certificate if we both go. Apparently, Nessa, the lady who owns the salon, is related to Dr. Cronus and Hermie, so it's not like we're going to see a stranger. And Mrs. Blain wants to go to the workshop tonight since she's into goddesses, so no one can object. Can't you see? This is exactly what we need."

Ruth was staring at me with her usual look of panic. "Who, me? Find my inner goddess?"

"Yeah, come on. It will be fun."

Ruth looked doubtful and began shaking her head.

"Oh, come on. *Please.* For me. I want to audition for the part of Tallulah, and she's a real goddess if ever there was one. I'm sure this is all meant to be." I got off the bed and went into one of Tallulah's song-and-dance routines. When I'd finished, she actually clapped!

"Hey, Gemma, you're really good," she said.

"Thanks. I've rehearsed enough times, that's for sure, and if I can find my inner goddess, I'm sure I'll make more of an impact, and I might get a part in the show. And you can find your inner goddess and be more confident."

"But I don't want to be a goddess or in the show."

I sighed. "You don't have to be in the show. I just thought . . . well, it would be nice to have someone to go to the workshop and the makeover with. Company. And you might get something out of it. And . . . and if you don't come with me, I can't go. Mrs. Blain said I could only go if you came and . . . no one else is going to come. They all have friends."

Ruth shook her head and put her headphones back on. "Sorry," she mouthed.

I got up off the bed and went to lie on my own. *Life stinks*, I thought as I turned to the wall. *It gives you a break. Then it takes it away.*

I felt close to blubbering mode. For a moment I'd had hope, and now it seemed like there was none left. I didn't know what else to do.

After a few minutes, I felt a hand on my shoulder.

"Okay," said Ruth as I turned around. "If it really means that much to you, I'll come with you. Not for a makeover or to be a goddess, but to keep you company. That's all."

"You're the best," I said and leaned over and gave her a hug. She looked nice when she smiled.

"Okay, my lovely goddesses, gather around," said

Nessa, the woman running the class.

Goddesses. I had to laugh. It was Thursday night, and as promised, Mrs. Blain had given us a lift to Pentangle. I'd been looking forward to it all day. I imagined that the class would be like a session at a modeling agency with tips on how to walk, how to get made up, hair advice, everything I'd need to land the part of Tallulah.

The décor in the salon was fabulous. It looked like a cross between Santaland at the mall and a planetarium, with planet mobiles spinning from the ceiling and star-shaped lights twinkling around the doors, arches, and mirrors. The assembled "goddesses," however, couldn't have looked less divine as we gathered in the manicure room at the back of the salon. The group was:

Mrs. Blain and her enormous bosom.

Ruth and her look of panic.

Me and my zits.

A stooped old lady who resembled a tortoise and had brought along her knitting.

A tiny red-haired girl who looked like she was going to burst into tears at any moment.

A tall girl with lank dark hair who was so pale that she looked like a ghost.

On the other hand, Nessa was pure goddess. Straight out of the pages of *Cosmo* magazine, she was glamorous and a half, in a Paris Hilton type of way. She was tanned, tall, and curvy, with long, highlighted blond hair, silver stars on her ears, and glittery nail extensions. She was dressed in figure-hugging white. A "hot mama," as Jess's brother used to say.

"Hey, y'all," she said in a slow Southern drawl as we gathered awkwardly around her. "As you know, this class is to find your inner goddess. All right?"

"All right," we said and nodded back.

I couldn't wait for it to begin. Nessa was so stunning to look at that I felt like a frump beside her. *But not for long*, I thought. If finding her inner goddess had helped her look the way she does, I'd come to the right place.

"Now, I want you to have a quick glance at your goddesses," she instructed, "and then we'll have the slide show."

I sat down and glanced at the paper I had been given, expecting to see all of the contemporary goddesses listed: Madonna, Britney Spears, Jennifer Lopez, Julia Roberts—all of the celebrities that we see on TV and in magazines. But no. It looked like a history-homework handout. Pages and pages of info: African goddesses, Asian, Himalayan, Greek, Roman, South American, North American, Egyptian, Hindu . . .

"Fascinating, isn't it?" said Mrs. Blain as she sat next me to and began to read. "I find these ancient entities so interesting."

"Um, yes . . ." I said as I glanced at my own sheet. The writing was a bit blurry, so it was hard to read, but I could just about make out some of the names:

Branwen. Lady of Love.

Cerridwen. Lady of Inspiration.

Hine-Moa. Passionate Princess.

Kura. Falling Flower.

Inanna. Queen of Heaven.

Allwise. Swan Maiden.

Some of the names sounded lovely, and I wondered which one was going to be my inner goddess as I scanned the sheet. I hoped that the slide show would be more informative, though. I wasn't really interested in lists of names from history. I was interested in the present.

A few minutes later, the lights went down, and the slide show began. *This will be it*, I thought. *She's probably going to show us how to glide on a catwalk. How to stand and move like a goddess.*

But no.

It was a slide show of a bunch of old statues and sacred sites.

"The power of these names," said Nessa, "and the power of the entities who once claimed these names has been forgotten; the devotion of the faithful considered odd, superstitious even . . ."

Strange, I thought as I listened. Nessa lost her Southern accent as she spoke, and she became more serene and authoritative. *All the same, I didn't come here for this.* Luckily, Mrs. Blain got out a bag of Skittles and passed it around, which provided some distraction. She was riveted by the talk, and even Ruth looked interested. I felt like nodding off. *Where's the makeup lesson?* I asked myself. *The top tips? Maybe this is just the beginning. We'll probably get going on the good stuff later.*

But no.

Nessa told us about the traditions, myths, and legends of goddesses in different countries throughout history. Not a word on how to apply lip gloss. *Peculiar,* I thought as I watched Nessa enthusing on about temples and sacred sites. She didn't look like the type to be into that sort of stuff, but she was clearly passionate about it.

After the slide show was over, Nessa asked us all to gather in a circle around a table with an open box on top of it.

"And now we're going to find our inner goddesses," she announced.

At last, I thought.

"I've put the names of all of the goddesses on pieces of paper in the box," she said. "Now I want you all to close your eyes and ask your inner goddess to direct your hand to the paper with your personal goddess's name on it. I'll go first."

She put her hand inside the box and pulled out a piece of paper.

"Greco-Roman goddess." She smiled and then smoothed her hands over her curves and winked. "Venus. Mistress of Love, Beauty, and Pleasure!"

"Quite right," said Mrs. Blain as Nessa turned to the old tortoise lady.

"Okay," she said. "Your turn, Betty."

Betty closed her eyes and put her hand inside the box.

"What's it say, darlin'?" asked Nessa, her Southern drawl back. "Read it out loud."

"I've got a Central American one," said Betty. "Ix Chel, the Lady Weaver."

"And that's just what you are, with your knitting," said Nessa with a nod. "Lydia, you're next."

The tall, pale girl closed her eyes and picked.

"Northern European goddess," she whispered. "Holda, the Host of the Dead."

Dead right, I thought. *She looks like someone only dug her up this morning.*

"Fantastic," said Nessa. "Don't look so glum, Lydia. Death often means rebirth in ancient myths. A new beginning." She indicated the box again. "Mrs. Blain?"

Mrs. Blain closed her eyes and picked.

"Like Betty," she said, "I've got a Central American one, too. Mayahuel." And then she chuckled and adjusted her bosom. "The many-breasted one!"

We all laughed. Once again, the name seemed apt.

"Mary," said Nessa, glancing at the little red-haired girl who looked like she'd been crying all day.

Mary took her turn and picked a piece of paper.

"Eastern European goddess. Bozaloshtsh. Lady Who Cries."

Wow! These are so accurate, it's scary, I thought. *I wonder which one I'll be.*

Nessa turned to Ruth. "What about you, Ruth? You going to give it a try?"

Ruth shook her head and looked at the floor.

Nessa smiled at her. "Come on, sweetheart. No one's going to pick on you. You're safe here. You're among goddesses."

Ruth hesitated and then got up and picked from the box.

"It's an Egyptian one," she said and smiled up at Nessa. "Seshat, the Mistress of Books."

Well, that definitely fits! I thought. *She's never got her nose out of one.*

"And last but not least," said Nessa, "Gemma."

I closed my eyes and put my hand inside the box. What would it be? Mistress of Flowers? Lady of the Spring? Swan Maiden?

"What's it say, darlin'?" asked Nessa as I read.

"South American goddess. Caipora," I said. I quickly folded up the paper and put it back on the table.

"And what's she the goddess of?" asked Mrs. Blain.

"Oh, nothing," I said.

"Can't be," insisted Mrs. Blain. "They're all the goddesses of something." She put her hand inside the box and found my paper and then burst out laughing. "Caipora. The Lady of the Beasts."

I felt myself turn bright red as everyone laughed with her. *Typical*, I thought. *There were some beautiful-sounding ones. Ladies of the moon, the forest, rivers, or the stars or the sea, but no, my inner goddess is the Lady of the stupid Beasts.*

I wished I hadn't come.

Chapter Seven
Showtime

Lunchtime. Friday.

Dear Diary,

Caipora, the Lady of the Beasts here. Gemini Zodiac crazy girl. That's me.

Life stinks. I'm pimply and ugly and everyone hates me. This week has been the worst ever since time began.

First I meet some weird motorcycle messenger named Hermie and he tells me that I'm a Zodiac Girl. He must be laughing so hard with his cousin Nessa or whatever relative she is. Maybe she's his girlfriend and they're in it together. I'm never listening to him again and have thrown his stupid cell phone in the Dumpster out back. It didn't work anyway, except to call him or the beauty salon. I tried putting all of my friends in the address book, but when I went to call them, the line was dead. What sort of dumb phone is that where you can only call two people?

And the stupid website he sent me to. Said I have a chance for one month because of some planetary alignments or something and could make my mark. My mark as what? Class geek?

And things are getting worse. Now I have three zits. One on my forehead, one on my chin, and one on the side of my nose.

And my hair has got a life of its own.

And even worse than *that*, I was in English today, and Mrs. Johnson asked me to read out loud, and when I couldn't because the page was blurry, she said I needed glasses, and I had to go and get my eyes checked by the school nurse in her clinic, and *she* said I needed glasses, too. So that's it. I'll be pimply, with glasses. And wild hair. There is no hope for me.

I've tried to get Ruth talking, but all she does is read and is the most boring roommate in the history of time. She loved the goddess class and has since gotten loads of books about them out of the library, which have given her even more excuses to have her nose permanently in a book. Which is fitting because she is the Lady of the Books. While I am the Lady of the Beasts. Clearly because that is what I look like. A beast. With glasses. And zits.

I WANT friends. I want to be beautiful. And cool. And to be Tallulah in the school show. And I want to be a Lady of Flowers. Not Beasts.

So there. The end. Amen. Everything stinks. I miss Lucy and Chloe and Jess and Charlotte and Ellie and have now used up a whole month's phone cards talking to them. And they all sound so happy and busy, like they have lives. I knew this would happen. I'm all alone in the world. With no one but my zits to keep me company. I wish, I wish, I wish I could play Tallulah. Auditions are this afternoon.

"Hey, Gemma," said Ruth, looking up from her book.
   "What?"
   "What are you doing?"
   "Writing in my diary. Why?"
   "Says here in my book that Caipora is a nice goddess. She's the protector of animals."
   "So?"
   "So I don't think you should mind that she's your inner goddess. I think you should be flattered. And I've seen that picture of your dog by your bed. Maybe you being the Lady of the Beasts means that you're a kind person who likes animals."
   You're a kind person, I thought. *Trying to make me feel better, but it isn't working.* I knew that I was the Lady of the Beasts because I looked like a beast.
   "Have you checked your site today?" asked Ruth. "There might be another message on it."
   "No way. I think that Hermie was having a laugh at my expense."
   "I thought the class was really good. And I liked

Nessa. I don't think she was laughing at you. Or any of us. Take a look."

"Well, I was just going to check my e-mail, so I guess I could have a peek before the auditions start," I said as I turned on my laptop. "Are you going to try for a part?"

Ruth shook her head. "I'm going to the outreach program. Apparently there are hardly any volunteers since everyone wants to be in the show. Sure you won't come?"

"Nah," I said. "Not my thing. What do you have to do?"

"Not much. Visit the nursing home at the bottom of the driveway and sit and read to them."

Well, that will suit Ruth and her books, I thought, *but I can't think of anything more boring.* I looked to see if there were any e-mails from Jess or the girls, but there was nothing. *Might have known. They're starting to forget about me already.*

I was just about to close down when a pop-up message flashed on from the astrology site.

"Not talking to you," I said as I stuck out my tongue at the screen and stood up from my desk.

Ruth got up from her bed and slid into my place.

"It says 'Lady of the Beasts,'" she read, "'protector of animals. Make your mark and find your calling; you have just over three weeks left.'"

"You're making it up," I said.

Ruth looked indignant. "Am not!"

I leaned over her, and sure enough, there were the words that she had read out. *This is getting freaky*, I thought as I quickly turned off the laptop. *What is going on? Now even my computer is making fun of me. Either that or Nessa told Hermie about the class and my being the Lady of the Beasts, and they both had a good giggle.*

I was late for the auditions, as the school nurse had been in touch with my mom and arranged for me to see the school's optician in the early afternoon. He confirmed that I needed glasses, and after testing my eyes, he let me pick a set of frames. Then he said that he'd make up a pair to my prescription and have them sent to the school. In the meantime, he gave me a temporary pair.

"You have got to be joking," I said when I looked at myself in the mirror. They looked like the bottom of soda bottles with enormous frames. "These are horrible. I look like a clown."

"It's only temporary," he said. "You make sure you wear them, young lady, or you'll be straining your eyes and damaging your eyesight. I don't want to hear that you've taken them off, except at night when you're asleep."

Yeah, yeah, I thought. *I've managed so far. I'll stick them in my bag as soon as I get out of here and wait until the half-decent ones arrive, because no way am I going to be seen dead or alive in these.*

"Don't worry," said the school nurse. "I'll make sure that everyone on staff knows that she has to have them on."

Is everyone at this school in league against me? I asked myself as I stumbled out of the room and headed for the drama department. *Don't they know that my destiny awaits and I have to get a part in the show?*

The auditions were already well under way by the time I got there, and the girls were in the middle of a dance routine. Mrs. Woods, the drama teacher, looked up and waved me toward her.

"Auditions for the part of Fat Sam are later," she said as she pointed me toward the benches at the back of the hall, where a group of girls was waiting.

I was aghast. "Fat *Sam*? No. I'm up for the part of Tallulah," I said. "I know all of her songs by heart."

"Tallulah? But we need a tall blond for Tallulah, and anyway, we auditioned for that part earlier. We're on to Blousey's part now."

Behind her, I could see Sara Jenkins and her friends waltzing around on their toes. I also noticed that Sara had been dancing nearby when Mrs. Woods had suggested that I play Fat Sam and had laughed and then passed it on to Mercedes.

". . . Yes," Mrs. Woods continued. "We'd have to pad you out a bit, but those glasses are a great idea. Inspired. I think you'd make a great Fat Sam in them. Where did you get them from? The props room?"

"No," I wailed. "The optician said I have to wear them, but not for long. With a blond wig, I could do Tallulah. Oh, please. Let me try."

"We haven't got time to go through it all again," said Mrs. Woods, who was beginning to look annoyed. "We've got a whole host of parts to cast."

"Then can I try for Blousey? I did put my name down. Please. Please."

Mrs. Woods sighed. "Very well, Gemma, but we've already been through the dance routine once, so just join in where you can. I'll soon see if it's right for you."

I quickly went to the back of the group and watched what they were doing. It was a different routine from the one we'd done when we did the show at my old school, but I studied it for a few minutes and then began to copy what the others were doing.

Easier said than done. They went one way, and I went the other. They'd had time to practice; I was thrown in at the deep end. Mercedes did a balletic leap backward as I pirouetted forward, and I ended up splayed on the floor with my ugly glasses askew on my nose.

"Oops," Sara said with a laugh.

Mrs. Woods clapped her hands for attention and motioned for me to get up. "Okay, girls, you can stop there. I think I've seen enough, and we've got to move along. I'll post my decision for Blousey later. Now then, those girls at the back who've been waiting, let's see who's right for the part of Leroy next. Okay, everyone who's auditioning, get up and come forward; the others take your places at the back."

I went to sit on the benches at the back and watched as six girls went through Leroy's routine.

"Love your glasses," said Sara with a snide look. "Going for the fishbowl look, are you?" Then she did what I can only assume was an imitation of a goldfish, opening and closing her mouth.

I didn't even bother to reply.

"Oh, you poor thing," said Mercedes. "It must be *so* hard, having to wear glasses."

I didn't reply to her either. I knew she was being sarcastic. A few minutes later, I heard her sing, "There once was an ugly duckling . . ." Then she laughed.

I felt like crying, but I bit my bottom lip and swallowed back my tears. I wasn't going to give them the pleasure of seeing how much they had upset me. Not if I could help it.

* * *

Later in the day, it was announced that Bugsy would be played by Mercedes, Tallulah by Sara, and Blousey by Lois.

I was offered a tiny part as an undertaker.

Over my dead body, I thought. *Social services and the outreach program, you've just got yourself another volunteer.*

Chapter Eight

Makeover madness

At last it was Saturday. Rest and relaxation and my first week in the school from Hades was over. Sadly, Mom and Dad weren't allowed to visit, because the school said that new students needed the first two weeks on their own to find their feet, but all visitors would be welcome the following Sunday. I didn't need to find my feet. I knew exactly where they were—on the end of my legs and ready to start walking out of there. I couldn't wait for Mom and Dad to come so that I could tell them how lonely it had been. Hopefully, they'd see sense and get me out and back to sanity. I couldn't wait.

For once, Ruth had her head out of a book and seemed to be getting ready to go out.

"Where are you going?" I asked.

"Oh. The salon," she replied. "Remember the gift certificate? Nessa booked us in this afternoon for the full treatment. She told us when we were leaving the goddess class."

I vaguely remembered Nessa saying something, but

hadn't paid too much attention. I was too upset with my inner beastie goddess person.

"Um . . . is that still all right with you?" continued Ruth. "You did say that I could use it. Um. Sorry."

"Ruth, you don't have to act like a scared mouse around me," I said. "Sure. Take the certificate. I won't be using it." *It will probably be another lecture on the ancient goddesses through time*, I thought, and I'd learned enough about them to last a lifetime.

Ruth sat at the foot of my bed. "Are you upset about yesterday?"

I shook my head. "Nah," I lied. "Win some, lose some."

"I think you'd have made a great Tallulah," said Ruth. "They don't know what they're missing."

Jess would have said exactly the same thing if she was here, I thought.

"Thanks," I said.

"I mean it. You'd have been great. So what are you going to do today?"

"Oh, stay here. Read. With these monstrosities of glasses, at least I can see now." Not that the idea of an afternoon by myself appealed that much; I just didn't want to be seen at the moment. I'd had about as much as I could take of being called four eyes or the ugly duckling by Sara and her sarcastic friends.

"Oh, please come with me," said Ruth. "It would

be nice to have company, and anyway, you can't hide away from the world up here. That's not the answer."

I had to smile when she said that. In one week, we'd done a complete turnaround. Now *she* was the one urging *me* to go out, while all I wanted to do was hide from the world under the covers.

Ruth got up from the bed and went to my laptop. "Let's see what the site says."

"You can," I said. "I'm really not interested. I mean, so much for being a Zodiac Girl. I thought it might have been a good thing, but now I think it's some kind of curse. Like, where's it gotten me? Nowhere."

Ruth pressed a few buttons on the keyboard. "There's a message for you. From Hermie. He says he's been trying to call you and that you can't give up. To trust him. And not to be oversensitive. He says Saturn will intervene to teach you a lesson, but Venus is still well aspected for a few more days, so make the most of it. Oh, come on, Gemma—come with me for the makeover. Please. It would be good to get away from school for a few hours."

"Pffft," I said as I looked out the window. "Stupid site. Saturn. Venus. Aspects. What's all that supposed to mean, anyway?"

However, it was a bright fall day. It would be a shame to stay inside. Everyone would be going into town on the school bus, and Ruth would be on her own among them. I ought to go, if only to protect her. She was such a mess. Her hair was back in its usual braid. She was out of uniform and dressed in a gray sacklike dress. She looked like she belonged to a past era more than ever.

"Okay, I'll come with you," I agreed. "Give me two minutes to put on my jeans."

Dr. Cronus was checking off names outside the main door in the courtyard, where the bus was waiting to take everyone into town.

"Jenkins, Peters, McMasters," he said with a nod as each girl passed him. "Whiting, Parker."

"Ah, there you are, fellow goddesses," Mrs. Blain called down from the front seat when she spotted Ruth and me. "Off for your makeover?"

I prayed that she'd keep her voice down, because Sara and her friends were at the back of the bus. The last thing I needed to get out was that I had an inner goddess—that I was Gemma, the Lady of the Beasts. They'd love it, and I'd never hear the end of it.

Dr. Cronus glanced up at Mrs. Blain and then rolled his eyes to the sky. "Goddesses? Makeover? Silly nonsense! You girls should be going to the library or to a bookstore. Doing something educational to enrich the mind and the soul, not wasting time on superficialities."

He can talk, I thought as I looked at his tie. If that wasn't silly, then I didn't know what was. The pattern of stars and planets against a bright blue background was a strange choice for someone who dressed so soberly most of the time. *I bet Hermie bought it for him*, I thought—the star pattern was like the one that Hermie had tattooed on his arm.

Mrs. Blain smiled back at him. "Not true," she said. "Life should be about balance, and the girls need some light relief. They work hard enough during the week and deserve a little downtime. And it's not all frivolous. We've been discovering our inner goddesses, haven't we, girls?"

"Has that Nessa been doing her goddess classes again?" Dr. Cronus frowned. Then he looked directly at me. "There's only one lesson you need to learn, young lady, and that's to love yourself and be yourself."

Yeah, right, I thought as I took a seat behind Mrs. Blain. Just shows what that old codger knows about anything. Love myself? I *hate* myself. And be myself? I'd rather be anybody but me.

Ruth sat beside me and nudged me. "Um . . . did you know that another name for Saturn is Cronus? I read that in my book about gods and goddesses."

"So?"

"Dr. Cronus. Don't you get it? The site said that Saturn would intervene to teach you a lesson."

"So?"

"So, Saturn, Cronus."

"She's quite right," said Mrs. Blain, turning around. "Gods and goddesses often have two names. Like Mercury. In some cultures, Mercury is known as Hermes."

Ruth nudged me again. "Hermes, Hermie."

"Yeah, yeah. And John is also known as Jack and Katherine as Kate," I said. "They're only names."

Ruth shrugged, but as we rode on, I began to wonder. Could it be possible that the planets were walking around in physical form? *Nah. Never in a million years. Crazy. I'm losing my mind,* I told myself as the welcome sight of stores came into view.

Nessa looked up from doing an old lady's hair and beamed when Mrs. Blain dropped us off at the salon.

"I wasn't sure you were coming," she said as she put the finishing touches on her customer. "Hermie said that he hadn't been able to reach you on your phone. But I'm so glad that you both made it. Be with you in two seconds—just got to finish off here."

While Nessa showed the lady the back of her hair in a mirror, the receptionist introduced Ruth to a beautician named Tracey who marched her off to a room at the back. While I was waiting, I sat down and flicked through a magazine.

"Cup of tea while you wait for your driver?" Nessa asked the lady, who smiled and nodded.

As Nessa disappeared into the back, the salon door clinked open. My heart sank when I saw Sara come in with Mercedes. I quickly ducked down to the side of the reception area, where I could see them but they couldn't see me. I shouldn't have worried. They weren't staying. Sara glanced around, took one look at the old lady in the chair, and then declared loudly, "Let's get out of here quick. Hairdos for the living dead."

Mercedes giggled, and out they flounced.

"You can come out now," called the old lady as soon as the door shut behind them.

I peeked my head up. "Oh, yes . . . right. Sorry. Just someone I didn't want to see."

"I can understand why," said the lady. "What *rude* girls."

"I know. Sorry about them," I said. "We're not all like that at our school."

"You're from Avebury, are you?"

I nodded and went to stand behind her. Although she looked like she was well into her 80s, her cornflower-blue eyes twinkled with life, and she was very elegant in a dove-gray suit, pearls around her neck, and her silver hair swept up at the back. I hoped that I looked as good as she did when I was her age.

"And . . . your hair looks lovely," I said. "Please

don't take any notice of them or listen to what they said. They can be really mean."

"Oh, don't you worry, dear," the lady said and then chuckled. "The living dead! Well, there's plenty of life left in this old girl, I can assure you. Just you wait and see."

"Here's your tea," said Nessa, who reappeared from the back carrying a tray with a china cup on it. "Now, is it okay if I leave you alone and get started with Gemma?"

"Of course. I'll be fine," said the old lady. "And thank you for the tea."

Nessa took me into a small treatment room next door to the one that Ruth was in, and once we were alone, she looked me up and down like I was a prize piece of meat.

"Hmm. Best get started," she said. "I like a challenge."

What nerve, I thought, but I knew what she meant. My hair was wilder than ever, and with my glasses, no one was going to look at me twice, except with pity.

She sent me off to a changing room at the back of the salon to put on a robe, and as I was getting undressed, I heard the front door open. *Probably the old lady's driver has come to pick her up*, I thought.

After that, I was pummeled and plucked and exfoliated and moisturized. At one point, I peeked in the mirror to see what Nessa was doing, only to see that she had covered my face with some pale green glop. I looked like a monster.

Nessa caught me looking and quickly covered the mirror with a huge white towel. "No peeking until I'm finished," she said as she produced a jar of cream. "Now. This is my mystery potion for blemishes. It's full of herbs from the Himalayas in India. They'll be gone in no time. Give me those glasses, and I'm going to pop out for a while to see what I can do. You stay here and let the face mask work its magic. Back in a jiffy."

I lay back on the reclining chair and prayed that she wasn't making fun of me and that I wasn't going to end up looking worse than I had before. *Nothing to lose,* I thought. *I might as well enjoy it.*

When Nessa came back, she painted my fingernails and toenails a cool glittery turquoise and then set about cutting my hair.

"Only one thing to do with hair like yours," she said. "We'll keep it long and put some layers in it. It will take the weight out of it."

"Whatever," I said. I was beginning to enjoy the experience. All of the lotions and potions smelled wonderful, of roses and jasmine, and I was starting to feel relaxed and lightheaded.

After the cut, she blow-dried my hair. "I'm going to straighten it to give it some shine," she said, "and I've got some great products for taking the kinks out, if you want. You can take them back to the school with you to use there."

"Whatever," I said again, but I was definitely feeling better. To have straight hair was my dream.

For the final touch, Nessa applied a little makeup.

"*Au naturel* for someone your age," she said, "but a little concealer for those blemishes, a touch of highlighter here, and a bit of blush there won't hurt, and it will bring out your coloring. You're a very lucky girl to have such gorgeous brown eyes."

Ha! I thought. *"Gorgeous" and "me." Not two words that usually go together.*

After a few hours, she had finished.

"Want to look?" she asked.

"Sure," I said. She couldn't have made me look worse. Nothing could.

She led me to the mirror that she had covered with the towel and then swished it away.

"Ta-dah," she said as I gazed at my reflection. "What do you think?"

I stared at the girl in the mirror. She looked *great*. I couldn't believe it.

"Is that me?" I asked.

"It certainly is," she said. "Every girl has it in her powers to be a frump or a goddess, and you, my dear Gemma, are definitely of the goddess variety."

"Wow," I said as I gazed at my reflection. "The Lady of the Beasts has been tamed."

"Exactly." Nessa beamed.

I really did look amazing. My hair was perfect, silky and soft to my shoulders, and Nessa had even put in some chestnut highlights.

I turned and gave Nessa a hug. "Thank you *so* much. I don't know how you did it."

"No problem, darlin'," she said with a smile. "But I only brought out what I saw."

Then I remembered something. "Oh, but I still have to wear my glasses. They're going to ruin all your hard work."

Nessa tapped the side of her nose. "When I do a makeover, I do a makeover, and nothing is going to ruin it. I've been over to see the optician, and he was just working on your prescription. I persuaded him to get a move on, so here they are. Try them."

I tried on the glasses, and as everything came into sharper focus, I looked back in the mirror. The glasses were perfect. They were an oval shape with no frames. Best of all, they had a slight rose tint, so they looked more like really cool sunglasses than eyeglasses. *No one will call me an ugly duckling in these.*

"And I've asked him to order you some contact lenses as well, so you have the choice," said Nessa. "Some days, you won't have to wear glasses at all."

"Nessa, you're a star," I said. For some reason, Nessa seemed to find this very funny and cracked up laughing.

"Private joke," she said. "That's a good one. Now let's see how Ruth's doing with Tracey next door."

We knocked on the door. "Just a sec," said Tracey before she opened the door.

"Omigod!" I said when I saw Ruth.

"Omigod!" said Ruth when she saw me.

She looked fabulous. Tracey had gotten rid of Ruth's braid and had cut her hair into shoulder-length layers. She'd even put in delicate blond highlights. Ruth no longer looked like a scared mouse. She looked very pretty. Fragile, but pretty.

"Ruth, you look amazing."

Ruth blushed. "Do I?"

"Take a look," said Nessa.

Ruth turned to the mirror, and her eyes almost popped out of her head. "Is that me?"

"Sure is, darlin'," Nessa said with a grin and gave the other beautician the thumbs-up. "Nice job, Trace."

When we got back on the bus, no one recognized us.

Nessa had pulled some clothes out of a chest at the back of the salon, and Ruth was now dressed in a pink, ripped, off-the-shoulder T-shirt with the words "Goddesses Rule" written on it and a cool pair of white jeans, as well as pink sneakers with silver stars on the sides.

She'd given me a pale blue T-shirt with the words "Bite Me" on it.

Sara Jenkins did a double take when she finally recognized us and nudged Mercedes, who was sitting next to her. Mercedes glanced over, and her eyes widened with shock.

"It's the ugly duckling," she said.

I made my arms float up like a ballet dancer about to fly. "Yes, but now I'm a swaaaannnnn!" I said as I flew past and took a seat at the back of the bus.

"More like a duck," said Sara sulkily.

And, at that moment, I understood something unbelievable. Sara was jealous.

Tasha turned around and smiled at me. "You look great, Gemma," she said. "And so do you, Ruth. Really pretty."

"Thanks." I smiled as I did my best to look modest.

Maybe being a Zodiac Girl had its pluses after all.

Chapter Nine

Clear as mud

After a dinner of chicken potpie and mashed potatoes on Saturday evening, I went out to retrieve my phone from the garbage area outside. I really wanted to thank Hermie for the makeover. It had worked wonders, not only with the way I looked, but also with the way people treated me. It had been fantastic when I got back to school; I'd been the center of attention and felt like a celebrity.

When I got outside the kitchen, to my horror, it looked like the Dumpsters had recently been emptied. All that was in one was a pile of broken eggshells and a mound of potato peels. As I was scrambling around, head in the trash, butt in the air, I heard someone call my name. *Oh, no,* I thought as I almost toppled in. *Please don't let Sara or Mercedes have seen me again.*

"Gemma," the voice called again. "I know you're in there."

I swung my legs back down and turned. It was Hermie, standing there with a big grin on his face. He was holding my phone.

"Looking for this?"

I felt sheepish. "Yes. Sorry. I threw it out when I was mad at you."

"So, the fact that you're looking for the phone, does that mean that you're not mad at me anymore?"

I nodded. "Yes. I mean no. Not mad. I wanted to thank you. We had a really good time with Nessa."

"I can see," he said. "You look great. I told you that Venus was well aspected. Happy now?"

I nodded again. "Yes . . . but . . ."

"But?"

"But . . . well, it was really cool getting all the nice comments and stuff when we first got back and everyone wanted to talk to me and find out where I'd had my hair done, but . . ."

"But?"

"But then they all went off, back into their own little groups of friends. And Ruth hated the attention and scuttled back upstairs, and here I am on my own again. I look great, but it hasn't really made any difference. I feel like Cinderella with no ball to go to."

"Friends take time," said Hermie gently.

"I know. I miss mine. And . . ."

"And?"

"And even though it was great to be made to look my best, I want people to like me for me, not because I've got a cool haircut. Your grandfather said something

93

like that to me before we went to the salon. Told me to be myself and learn to love myself."

Hermie chuckled again. "Did he now? Sounds like the sort of thing he'd come out with. Yeah. Be yourself. Hard lesson, but then that's what Grandpa is all about. And he's right—learn to love yourself—but it doesn't mean that you have to go around looking like the back end of a bus, hon. Part of loving yourself is taking care of yourself. And Grandpa could definitely use a haircut."

I laughed, and we went to sit on a wooden bench under the copper beech tree to the right of the Dumpsters.

"How are you settling in otherwise, Gemma?"

"Not sure. This week has been . . . different . . . for all sorts of reasons. Not sure if I want to stay."

"It's early," said Hermie. "Don't give up. You're not a quitter. I know from your chart that it's a hard time for you at the moment. Some heavy aspects. A real turning point, but you could do something good here. It's all in your horoscope."

"Yeah, I got your message. How can you know all that? Just who are you, really? And one month to make my mark. But how? One week is already over. What does it *really* mean to be a Zodiac Girl?"

"It means what you make of it."

"Herm*ieeeeee*! What does *that* mean?"

"It means that life can throw all sorts of things at you, but it's what you make of it that matters. Like the way Nessa made you look your best—she was only bringing out what was already there. It's all about choices. Win or quit, sink or swim, gorgeous or frump, goddess or geek."

"You're talking in riddles."

"No, I'm not. Life is what you make of it. Choice. Choice. Choice. Can't say it enough times . . ."

"Um . . . you can, actually," I said, but I think he knew that I was joshing him.

"Some people hide away . . ." he continued.

"Like Ruth."

"Yeah. Like Ruth. Others get out there and rise to all the challenges, ride all the difficulties. Flight or fight. We both know what you do normally."

"Yeah, normally, I fight or swim or whatever. But this week has been anything but normal. I feel like I've lost sight of myself lately. Although . . . Gemini, that's the sign of the twins, isn't it?"

Hermie nodded.

"Well, maybe that's it," I said. "I have one twin who has crazy hair and is moody and oversensitive, and the other has nice hair and is a fighter. So I'm both—the one who fights *and* the one who runs away. The one who swims *and* the one who sinks. It's not easy having multiple personalities, you know."

Hermie laughed. "Everyone has days when they feel like running away. But maybe now it's time to let the fighter twin have a say." He got up and went over to his motorcycle. "Be the fighter you naturally are. Your chart is not the chart of someone who takes anything lying down. Your chart says you're a winner, and for this one month, heavy aspects, lessons to be learned and all, you *can* make things happen. It's a really special time for you. Anyway, got to go. Got messages to deliver. Stay cool."

As he rode away, I stared after him. He was a strange person. Kind and helpful one minute, confusing and restless the next. But appearing out of the blue sometimes, like a guardian angel or a fairy godmother. *Most peculiar*, I thought as my phone beeped.

It was the man himself.

"Forgot to say. The outreach program," Hermie said. "There are a lot of lonely people out there who need friends, and not just in schools."

"What do you mean?"

"Lady of the Beasts, you'll figure it out."

I raced back upstairs to find Ruth.

"Hey, Ruth, can I look at your book on the gods and goddesses?"

"Sure," she said and pulled down a heavy book from her shelf and onto the bed.

I sat on her bed and looked in the index at the back. I soon found the page that I wanted.

"You were right, Ruth," I said. "Saturn, sometimes known as Cronus. Often depicted in mythology as an old man. Saturn is the taskmaster. That's another way of saying the giver of lessons, isn't it? Sound familiar?"

"Sounds exactly like Dr. Cronus," said Ruth, looking over my shoulder. "Look up Mercury."

I flicked back through the pages and then read. "Mercury, also known as Hermes. Omigod. And listen to this. Grandson of Saturn."

We both looked at each other.

"Mercury. The planet of communication, often portrayed as the winged messenger," said Ruth, reading the rest of the page.

"And Hermie is a motorcycle messenger," I said.

"And Nessa is?" asked Ruth breathlessly.

"Exactly what I was thinking. Goddess of love and beauty. Hermie said that Venus was well aspected in my chart, and next thing we know, we meet Nessa. Coincidence or what? She runs a beauty salon, and she looks like a goddess. Venus. Nessa could be a nickname for Venus."

"Yeah . . . maybe," said Ruth.

"Yes, maybe," I said. "And she cracked up when I said that she was a star. Said it was a private joke.

Just who are these guys?"

"Call Hermie and ask," said Ruth.

"I will. Mercury rules Gemini. Mercury is the guardian of all Geminis. This is too weird. What sign are you, Ruth?"

"Taurus, but that doesn't mean that I'm a Zodiac Girl."

I went back to the book. "Taurus is ruled by Venus. You really got along with Nessa, didn't you?"

Ruth nodded. "I liked her. And I felt like she genuinely liked me. She was kind to me. I felt safe with her."

"Could it be . . . ? Do you think that maybe she's really Venus, here on Earth in bodily form?"

Ruth looked doubtful. "Dunno. There's got to be a rational explanation. It could be something really simple. People choose names for all sorts of reasons. All names have other meanings—like mine, Ruth, means compassion."

"And my name means gem or jewel. I remember my mom said she picked it because I was like a jewel in her life. Cheesy, huh?"

Ruth smiled. "Yeah, but sweet. Maybe the fact that Hermes and Cronus are the names of planets doesn't mean anything. They're just names. Maybe their family is into planets and stuff like other families are into baseball or basketball and name all of their kids after famous players. It might not mean anything."

"Yeah, I guess," I agreed. *That explanation makes sense*, I thought, but something was niggling me. There was something strange about it all. I was sure that there was more to it than just a coincidence over names. Ruth was clearly thinking the same thing.

"Do you think they could be, like, guardian angels or something?" she asked.

I laughed. "I wondered that. But Hermie isn't the guardian-angel type. He has tattoos."

"So?" asked Ruth. "Who says what they should look like? In my books I read that the ancient people always used to believe that the planets and stars took human form. Like, Zeus, the king of the gods, supposedly lived on a mountain in Greece. I mean, when you think about it, we don't really know who anybody is, do we? There might be lots of people walking around who are more than just people."

My brain was beginning to spin. "You've been reading too many books."

"I guess," said Ruth. "But we don't know a lot about who we really are, do we? I remember my grandma always used to say that there are old souls and young souls on this planet. She said that the young souls were usually the stupid ones, like bullies who cause trouble. Whenever we'd see a fight between drunk people or something on the news, she'd say, 'Huh, it's clearly *their* first time on the planet.' So if there can be old souls and new souls, maybe there can be people who are from the planets. I mean, none of us knows where we've *really* come from anyway, do we?"

I laughed. "In that case, I'd say you're an old soul, and Sara and her friends are new souls. But who knows? There are so many things I don't understand. Like this whole zodiac thing. I don't have a clue what it's really about."

"Ask Hermie," suggested Ruth. "If he is the real Hermes, then he's supposed to be the great communicator. So get him to communicate."

I pressed his number and got through a moment later.

"Hey, Hermie. I have to know, what does it mean to be a Zodiac Girl?"

"You asked that already and I told you—what you make of it."

"You *told* me *that* already."

"Okay, then. Different things to different girls," said Hermie. "Depends on the circumstances. Depends on the individual."

"That's so vague, Hermie. It doesn't mean anything."

"Maybe not at the moment. And to tell you the truth, some girls have been Zodiac Girls and haven't done a thing with the opportunity. Others have gone on to do great things. Like Joan of Arc—she was a Zodiac Girl. Madame Curie. What do you think got her started?"

"What?"

"She was a Zodiac Girl, and she went for it, big-time. Most of the great heroines in history were all Zodiac Girls."

"So why isn't Ruth a Zodiac Girl?"

"Not her turn. It's not in her chart at the moment. You never know. Her time may come later."

"So what am I supposed to do?"

"You'll figure it out. I can only tell you the influences that you're under this month."

"I don't know what you mean. Why can't you do magic or something and make it really clear?"

Hermie chuckled. "The magic's all around you, Gemma—just open your eyes. This planet you're on. It's a three-dimensional light show with a million smells, sounds, tastes, and feelings. It hangs, a jewel in deep space, turning on its axis each day. What could be more magical than that? And a sun that shines down on us, the Moon, the stars, a sky that goes on and on for light-years? What more could you want?"

"I don't know. Someone to make sense of it all."

"Gemma, relax. This time is yours, your chance to

make your mark. Be yourself. Be your best self. Go along with the outreach program. The way will become clearer."

It feels as clear as mud at the moment, I thought as he clicked off.

Chapter Ten

Chiron House

On Sunday, as half the school went into rehearsals, Ruth and I got ready to go to Chiron House for our first visit on the outreach program. We trooped down the stairs to join the group of volunteers waiting in the hall, and I felt a stab of envy as I saw all of the other girls excitedly on their way to rehearse *Bugsy*.

"Now, I want you all to be on your best behavior," said Mrs. Blain as she led us down the school driveway. "And be especially nice, as one of them is one of our school's main benefactors. We don't want to upset her, do we?"

"No, Mrs. Blain," we all chorused back.

"I'm not sure that I'll know what to do," said Ruth. "I've never done anything like this before."

"It'll be fine," I said. "Like with my grandma, she likes to ramble on about her childhood or her operations. It'll be no biggie. Just listen patiently, nod now and then, and you probably won't need to say anything. You could even wear your iPod for all they know. Okay?"

Ruth smiled and gave me the thumbs-up. But she

didn't look so sure as Chiron House loomed into sight in front of us.

"Wow. It's amazing in here," whispered Ruth as we walked into the reception room and took in the heavy curtains, acres of plush cream carpets, and displays of flowers that looked like they would cost most of my allowance for a year.

"I know," I whispered. "It's like a five-star hotel, only better. No expense spared. They must be very rich old ladies to be in a place like this."

"Well, Mrs. Blain did say that one of them was a big-time benefactor of the school," said Ruth. "Hope I don't get her. I'm bound to put my foot in my mouth."

Across the reception area, Mrs. Blain was talking to a sour-faced woman with thinning red hair who was dressed in a pristine white uniform.

"She looks like a barrel of laughs—not," I said, nudging Ruth.

Ruth glanced over and suppressed a giggle.

The woman turned toward us and shot us an icy smile.

"Welcome, girls," she said. "I'm the supervisor, Nurse Stepford, and my ladies are expecting you, but before we go in, I want to outline the rules. One," she said and flicked a bony finger and narrowed her eyes. "No raised voices, *ever*." And another digit was wagged in front of our noses. "Two. No running around, *ever*."

I threw a quick glance at Ruth, but she seemed to be hypnotized by the perfectly manicured red talons on the end of the two fingers wagging close to her face.

Then a third finger stabbed the air. "And three. Stay in the parlor. No wandering off anywhere under any circumstances. *Ever*. Any questions?"

Who does she think we are? I thought. *A bunch of children?*

Ice Nurse gave me a laser look, as if she'd read my mind.

"Okay, line up here," she barked and proceeded to meticulously inspect our hands. "Hmm. They seem reasonably clean," she said, sounding disappointed.

Once we'd been given the okay, she led us down a long corridor lined with portraits of scowling women.

"Hope we don't meet them," I whispered to Ruth, who snorted loudly. Nurse Stepford stopped in her tracks and asked her if she was feeling well.

"I'm fine. J—Just a frog in my throat," she blustered.

"Well, make sure it stays there. I want nothing upsetting my ladies," said Nurse Stepford, arching one eyebrow.

"I've heard of the ice maiden and the ice man, but now here cometh the ice nurse," I whispered, making Ruth laugh again.

Nurse Stepford opened a set of glass double doors, and we filed silently through to meet our ladies. One of them I recognized as the woman I'd met briefly in Pentangle salon, and she gave me a smile when I waved at her. There were eight others slumped in enormous chintzy armchairs around the room. They looked like a collection of wrinkled rag dolls. Some were reading and one in the corner was knitting, but most were just staring into space. *God, they look so bored*, I thought. *Like zombies in a five-star prison.*

Nurse Stepford began to assign each of us to a lady.

"You, off to see Mrs. Hamilton," she said to Ruth, pointing her in the direction of the lady from the salon. "That's her in the corner there."

Next, Rose, Imogen, and Grace got their ladies. Then Nurse Stepford looked down her nose at me.

"Now you," she said, looking at me as if I were some nasty bacterium. "Name?"

"Gemma Whiting, ma'am."

"Don't you 'ma'am' me, young lady," she snapped. "Call me Nurse Stepford."

I had to suppress a giggle as I imagined her saying, "Call me sir."

"Okay, Miss Whiting, you can go to Mrs. Compton-Grime," she said, nodding toward a small, plump lady who was studying a knitting pattern.

She must be well into her eighties, I thought as I looked

over the old lady's wiry white hair, bullfrog eyes, and thin red lips.

"Hello," I said with a smile as I approached her and looked around for somewhere to sit. "I'm Gemma."

She didn't look up.

"Um . . . is there anything I can do for you?"

"Yes. Scram," she said and clicked her needles viciously.

"Excuse me?" I asked, hardly believing what I had just heard.

"You heard me. Scram. I don't want anyone near me, especially an annoying little brat like you."

But I haven't even done anything to be annoying, I thought. I didn't know what to do or say next, so I looked around to see if anyone else had gotten a similar rejection. But no, everyone else seemed to be getting along fine, and Mrs. Hamilton and Ruth appeared to be having a real laugh together.

"Um . . ." I began again.

"What! You're still here?" snapped Mrs. Compton-Grime, finally looking up. "Can't you see I'm busy?"

"Um, yes, I've come . . . I'm with . . ."

"Spit it out, girl. Don't they teach you how to speak properly at your school?" she growled.

"Yes. I mean . . ."

"What, pray, brings you here to disturb this

sanctuary of peace and quiet?"

"Part of the outreach program at school. We visit people. Do good, that sort of thing."

"Why?" she asked, staring at me over her thick round glasses.

Good question, I thought. *Maybe I should have taken the part of the undertaker in* Bugsy. *Anything would be better than this.*

Mrs. Blain spotted my situation and came rushing over.

"Everything all right?" she asked.

"No," said Mrs. Compton-Grime. "This nasty child is very irritating. Please take her away."

I looked helplessly at Mrs. Blain.

"But . . . but . . . but . . ." I stammered.

"Remove her from my presence, NOW!"

Her raised voice caused Nurse Stepford to look over and scowl at me.

"Come on, Gemma," said Mrs. Blain. "Mrs. Compton-Grime doesn't want to be visited today. Why don't you go and join Ruth with Mrs. Hamilton?"

I couldn't move fast enough and was soon on the other side of the room. *Now I've blown it*, I thought. Judging by the way that Mrs. Blain was fussing over Mrs. Compton-Grime and apologizing, she was clearly the school benefactor.

Mrs. Hamilton smiled up at me. She pulled a pillow out from behind her back and threw it on the floor.

"Take a perch," she said. "Sorry we don't have enough chairs to go around, but you're a young thing—you'll be okay on the carpet."

I dutifully sat at her feet, next to Ruth.

Mrs. Hamilton leaned over close to my ear. "Don't you worry about that old battle-ax," she whispered.

"She said I was annoying," I said. "And I'd hardly opened my mouth."

"Silly old goat," said Mrs. Hamilton, reaching out for a gold box next to her chair. "Just because she's old, it doesn't mean that she's nice. Here, dear, have a chocolate. Some things never change, you know. Like you have those mean girls at your school. Same in here. There are the good, the bad, and the ugly everywhere."

"Tell me about it," I said and sighed as I helped myself to a Belgian caramel cream.

And she did. She was hilarious. She told us all about the other "inmates," as she called them, and how one had a habit of leaving her teeth in the fridge overnight so that they were cool in her mouth in the morning. Another was a sleepwalker who regularly had to be rescued from the rosebushes in the garden and one night from the fishpond. Another unfortunate lady thought that Nurse Stepford was her daughter and kept asking her if she had swallowed something nasty, because she always looked so sour. She also called Nurse Stepford "Betty," which she didn't like, as her name was Marjorie.

After half an hour of hilarious stories, Mrs. Hamilton said, "Okay, now it's your turn. Tell me all about school."

We bombarded her with tales of the bonkers teachers and the yucky school food and our fellow students' foibles. I even told her about Sara and her gang and how mean they could be, but how I'd answered back a few times. Mrs. Hamilton seemed to lap it all up and laughed out loud so often that the Ice Nurse came over to see if she was all right. By the time we had to leave, I felt like we were old friends.

"Do come again," she said, squeezing my hand when I got up to go. "I've really enjoyed today and meeting you and Ruth. I only arrived last week, and I'm bored out of my mind already. I enjoy a good laugh, and they are few and far between around here." Then she winked and said, "I guess the problem is, it's full of old people."

"Not you, though," I said and winked back.

"Is there anything we can bring you next time?" asked Ruth.

"Oh, anything to liven the place up a bit. I'm sure you'll think of something. We're not dead yet, you know, but the way we get treated, sometimes you'd think that we were."

Chapter Eleven

Planet deli

The following week, I began to feel more confident about figuring out my way around school and finding where my classes were. I buried my head in my schoolwork and tried not to think anymore about friends and whether or not I was liked. I also chose to ignore the strains of *Bugsy Malone* that echoed in the school corridors every night as everyone in the show went into rehearsal mode. Instead, I tried to focus on what was good in my life. Ruth was beginning to open up, and I found that beneath her shy appearance was a sweet and generous person. So she wasn't like Jess and my old friends—but, then again, no one could ever take their place.

Every day I checked the site to see if Hermie had sent anything interesting for my second week as a Zodiac Girl, but there was nothing there that made much sense to me. Just a list of predictions that could have been written in Greek for all the sense they made to me.

Monday: Mercury and Pluto are in a rare state of harmony.

Well, hooray for them, I thought, but the day did go smoothly, and Rose, Imogen, and Grace asked me to be on their team in a history quiz. And Tasha moved over in assembly so that I could take my place next to her. Sara didn't look too happy about that, though.

Tuesday: The Moon is well aligned with Jupiter, resulting in a fruitful time.

There was fruit salad after dinner, so maybe it meant that.

Wednesday: The Sun is linked to Uranus, so expect the unexpected.

I slipped on a newly washed floor on the way to math. That was unexpected. I felt like an idiot.

Thursday: Saturn and Mercury form an uneasy alignment.

I did have a run-in with Sara when she asked me where my pet mouse was, meaning Ruth. I told her that I didn't have a pet mouse, but I had seen a rat coming out of her room yesterday. It wasn't a very pleasant encounter.

Friday: Another harmonious lineup with Pluto and the Sun.

It was an okay day. In the afternoon, Mrs. Blain gave us a run-through of our duties for the next visit to Chiron House and told us to think of something we could take, but that was all.

Saturday: Jupiter is in a generous mood.

Good for him, I thought as I got ready to go into town with Ruth for our weekly outing.

"My parents sent me some money," she said with a shrug as we went down to catch the bus. "Guilt money. So let's go and spend it!"

"Cool," I said. "Jupiter rocks, I guess."

Ruth gave me one of her "you're-a-very-strange-person" looks, but I could tell that she was starting to like me more. She didn't hide in her books as much anymore, and sometimes she even said as much as two sentences.

"Zodiac messages," I said, by way of explanation. "Jupiter is in a generous mood, apparently. I still don't quite know what to make of it all, though. Like, is this it? Went to a goddess workshop, got my hair done, and got some cool products to keep it straight. Then

Hermie said to join the outreach program, and although it was nice meeting Mrs. Hamilton, I can't help thinking, so what? Is that all I get to achieve as a Zodiac Girl? A volunteer with nice hair who visits nursing homes?"

"It's only been two weeks," said Ruth. "Maybe the best is yet to come."

Or the worst, I thought. The first two weeks hadn't exactly been smooth sailing.

We had a lovely afternoon, though, browsing the stores and trying on clothes and makeup, and Ruth insisted on paying for treats like hot chocolate and pastries in a Greek deli on the main street. We chose it out of all of the other restaurants because it was called Europa, like our house back at school. I felt bad about Ruth forking out for everything because I didn't have a lot of extra money and wanted to spend what I did have on phone cards to call my old friends, but Ruth didn't seem to mind.

"What else am I going to do with the money?" She grinned as she dug into her pastry. "Just call me Jupiter."

"Oh, *noooo*," I groaned. "Don't tell me that you're one of them, too."

"Nope," she said and then made her eyes go cross-eyed. "Just me. Quite normal."

At that moment, the deli owner came over with

a plate of sumptuous-looking cakes that he put in front of us.

"On ze house," he said with a Greek accent as he stroked his expansive belly and smiled. "Eat. *Eat.* I'm in a generous mood today."

I couldn't resist. "Your name's not Jupiter by any chance, is it?"

He looked taken aback, but he quickly recovered and then laughed. "Most people call me Joe, but if you want to call me Jupiter, iz fine by me."

After he'd left, I nudged Ruth. "Did you see the apron he was wearing?"

Ruth nodded. "Same pattern as Hermie's tattoo."

"And Dr. Cronus's tie and Nessa's earrings," I said.

"And the deli is called Europa, which as we know from school is . . ."

"One of the four moons of Jupiter!" I finished for her.

Ruth looked over at the friendly deli man. "Hmm. Joe—Jupiter. I wonder if he's one of them, too? Wouldn't mind having him as my guardian if he is. Look at all the cakes."

I laughed. "Yeah. Slightly more appealing than a guy with tattoos and a motorcycle."

"Speaking of which," said Ruth. "Eyes left."

Hermie had just parked his motorcycle outside. He entered the deli a moment later.

"Hi," he called to Joe and then turned to us. "I see you've met my dad?"

Ruth and I looked at each other and almost choked.

"How many planets are there in astrology?" I asked Hermie as he sat at the table next to us.

"Nine," said Joe, bringing over a plate of ham-and-cheese sandwiches to give to Hermie. "Earth, Venus, Mercury." He winked at Hermie at this point, "Jupiter, Mars, Neptune, Saturn, Uranus, and Pluto."

"And could it . . . is it possible . . . do you think that maybe those planets might be here in human form?" I asked. "Like in the old days in ancient Greece?"

Joe stroked his chin. "Veeeery interesting question," he said and then turned to Hermie. "This iz your Zodiac Girl, yes?"

Hermie nodded.

"Bright kid," said Joe, and then he went back behind the counter, where he looked like he was chuckling to himself.

"So?" I asked Hermie.

"So what?" he replied.

"So are you guys the embodiments of the planets or not?"

"Complicated. Not exactly that simple," he said and then grinned, put his arm out, and flexed his muscles. "Though people do say that I have a heavenly body."

Joe cracked up laughing behind the counter.

"So are you going to tell me anything?" I insisted.

Hermie shook his head. "Maybe. What would you like to hear?"

I felt like throttling him. He never gave me a direct answer.

"*Anything.*"

"Only got one message for you today, chick," he said. "Mercury is going to go retrograde for a week."

"Meaning?"

"Mercury is the planet of communication, so when it goes retrograde, there are often mix-ups with communication. Misunderstandings. Computers crashing. Technology breaking down. Messages misplaced. Thought I'd better come and tell you before it all started happening."

"But is it going to be a good week or a bad week?"

"Depends on what you make of it," he said as he wolfed down his sandwich and then got up to go. "Anything could happen."

"Hermieeeeeeee! You're doing it again. Being vague. Not really telling me *anything*."

Hermie smiled a kilowatt smile. "You'll be fine. Just keep fighting and never give up. Going retrograde, it's nothing to worry about . . . I don't think. As I told you before, life is what you make of it. Catch you later."

Somehow, I didn't feel reassured.

Chapter Twelve

Lady of the Beasts

"Omigod," I heard Mercedes say as Dad's old van chugged its way up the driveway. "Have you seen the state of that?"

I went and stood close to her in the courtyard, where a crowd of girls was waiting for their parents. I was only expecting Dad, as Mom had called early that morning to say that she couldn't make it. She'd come down with some flu bug and sounded terrible.

"I know. It's fantastic, isn't it?" I said. "Vintage model. *Very* rare. Only one left in the whole world."

Tasha laughed, but in a nice way. She was laughing *with* me, while Sara, Mercedes, and Lois were always laughing *at* me.

"And have you seen that *thing* in the front?" sneered Sara.

I looked over at the van. Sitting in the passenger seat, with his nose out the window, was the best sight I'd seen all week.

"Bertie!" I cried.

Sara rolled her eyes up to the sky. "You'd better not bring that disgusting thing anywhere near me," she said. "I'm allergic to animal fur, and he looks like he needs a bath."

"Bertie's very clean," I said. "And he's not a thing—he's a dog."

Bertie looked in my direction and yelped with delight. Dad opened the door for him, and, with his tail wagging like crazy, he shot over to me and tried to jump up into my arms.

"He looks a little like you. Is he your brother?" asked Sara. "I can see the family resemblance with all that crazy hair."

I'd had enough. There was no reason for her to be so horrible to me, and I'd done my best to be friendly to her and her friends. I'd decided that I wasn't going to put up with it any longer. *Be yourself,* Dr. Cronus had said. *Be the fighter you naturally are,* Hermie had said. I was going to be that. The fighter. I never used to let people walk all over me at my previous school, but I had lost myself for a while when I'd arrived at this one. Thanks to Ruth and Nessa and Hermie, I'd found myself again. And I'm not the victim type. I am a Zodiac Girl, the Lady of the Beasts. *Grrr.*

I leaned on one hip and looked at her with pity. "Sara, he's a *dog.* A D. O. G. Haven't you ever seen

119

one before, or are you stupid? Who in their right mind would actually think that he's my brother? That's pathetic. But maybe I shouldn't embarrass you. It isn't your fault that you don't have one brain cell in that empty head of yours. In fact, your head is so empty that if someone shined a flashlight in your ear, your eyes would light up."

Sara's jaw dropped. She turned red and for a moment looked lost for words.

"Get lost, um . . . um . . . pig for . . . um . . ." she managed to finally stutter.

"Pig for what, Sara?" I asked. "For breakfast? For lunch? For brains? Come on—spit it out. What are you trying to say?"

"Oh, never mind," said Sara and flounced off with Lois.

Mercedes linked arms with Tasha. "Well, you might have had your hair done," she said, "but you still haven't got any friends here."

"Yes, I do," I said. "I have Ruth." I was beginning to like Ruth. She wasn't exactly the life of the party like my old friends, but she was a gentle soul, and there was something about her that made me want to take care of her. Like this morning, I felt really sorry for her. Since her parents were overseas on a year's contract, she wouldn't be having any visitors. I invited her to spend the day with Dad and me, but she shook her head and said that she'd be in the way, and nothing I could do would reassure her that she wouldn't be. But she looked so small and sad curled up on her bed on her own.

"Pfff," said Sara, turning back. "That mouse."

"Better than being a witch like some people," I said.

Sara looked shocked, but Tasha looked like she was going to laugh. As Mercedes pulled Tasha away, I noticed that Tasha yanked her arm out of her grasp. As she did, she turned back to me and mouthed, "Sorry."

Dad soon joined Bertie, and I gave him the grand tour of the school and filled him in on my first two weeks. The edited version. I'd been thinking a lot since the day before and wasn't so sure that I wanted to leave anymore. I was feeling stronger. Better. I wanted to give it a while longer. And it wasn't only because I'd had a makeover. It did feel great to look better and have some admiring glances and comments, but it was still the same me, straight or frizzy hair. Nerdy glasses or cool ones, it was still me inside looking out of them. I didn't want people to like me because I looked okay. I wanted people to like me because of who I am. Inside. Suddenly it didn't seem like such a big deal that I hadn't gotten in with Sara and Co. I wondered why I'd been so bothered about what they thought. I didn't even *like* them, although I was beginning to think that Tasha might be okay if she wasn't with Sara. There were other girls in the school who weren't unkind. It might take some time to get to know them all, but I didn't want to quit just because some mean girls had picked on me.

After the tour, we had coffee and Danishes in the dining room with the other visitors. As we were eating, Dad's cell phone rang, so he got up to take the call.

"Gemma," he said when he came back moments later, "would you mind if I left you for a couple of hours? I can come back later to have dinner with you. It's just that there's been an emergency, and I'm the closest mechanic. A car's broken down on the highway, and they need help. It's only fifteen minutes from here, so I could run out, do the repairs, and then be back."

"I could come with you," I said. I wanted to spend as much time as possible with him, but he wasn't listening. He was scanning the room for someone.

"Hey, where's Bertie?" he asked.

"Maybe asleep under a table somewhere. You know what he's like."

We searched all the spots where he could possibly have hidden, but he was nowhere to be found.

"Oh, dear," said Dad as he looked at his watch. "I have to get going soon. I can't leave people stranded on the side of the road. I hope Bertie hasn't gotten into any mischief. Where *is* he?"

We decided to split up to search for him, and I offered to look outside. It had started raining, so I went upstairs to get a jacket. When I opened the bedroom door, Ruth glanced up and beamed at me. There, sitting in her lap, was Bertie, and he and Ruth looked like the oldest of old pals.

"He's gorgeous," she said as Bertie gave her face a lick. "I knew it was him from your picture.

"But where . . . ? How did he get up here?"

"I went down to get a drink, and to avoid seeing everyone, I went through the drama department. I thought I heard Sara and her friends coming, so I hid in the props room until they'd gone past, and there he was, asleep on top of a pile of costumes. I brought him up here, and . . . I think he likes me."

"He almost gave my dad a heart attack," I said and laughed. "Dad had visions of him in the kitchen stealing tonight's dinner. I had visions of him chasing Boris!"

Ruth shook her head. "No. Nothing like that. He's been very good. He's a really special dog."

As she sat there petting him, I thought that I hadn't seen her so happy in all the time I'd known her. And then something hit me. Suddenly, I knew what it meant that I was the Lady of the Beasts.

"Ruth," I said. "I've just had the *most* fantastic idea."

Chapter Thirteen

Darned dog

Ruth looked horrified. "Keep Bertie here? But you know there are no dogs allowed. Where? How? For how long?"

"We can keep him in here. We can sneak food up to him. It's only for a few hours."

Ruth was shaking her head. "No. We'll get into real trouble."

"I'll take responsibility if we get caught, and it's only until later."

"But why? What difference is a few more hours going to make?"

"All the difference. Remember the outreach program? The visit to Chiron House?"

Ruth nodded. "Yes. I'm going later."

"So am I, now that Dad's leaving for the afternoon. And remember Mrs. Blain said that we had to take something with us when we visit?"

Ruth's jaw dropped. "She meant take a book or a cake or something. Not an *animal*. Not *Bertie*! Are you out of your mind?"

"No. I've never been more sure about anything.

It's the right thing to do. I saw a show on TV over the summer about using animals as therapy. It was amazing. They have great results with people in nursing homes. People who never spoke opened up, and others who were very sad became happier, and . . . and it lowers blood pressure—and good stuff like that."

"But . . ."

"No *but*s, Ruth. When I saw you with Bertie just now, it all clicked into place. What I'm supposed to do. And I'm sure that this is what Hermie's been hinting about—you know, the Lady of the Beasts, join the outreach program, saying that there are lonely people everywhere, not just in schools. Don't you see? It's *obvious*! He meant the old ladies."

Ruth shook her head, but her lack of enthusiasm didn't put me off. I knew that taking Bertie to the nursing home and starting my own animal-therapy program was what I was supposed to be doing. Thanks to Nessa, I now knew that it was my calling as the Lady of the Beasts.

"Dad's got to go and fix a car that's broken down, so he'll be gone a while. It's too perfect. Like fate made a car break down so that Dad would have to leave Bertie here. It will be great. If anyone knocks, shove Bertie in the closet, and if he barks, cough like crazy, like you've got a terrible cold."

"Whoa. Gemma. Calm down. Think this through. I mean, *fate*?"

I felt dizzy with excitement. "Yes! Fate! Destiny is calling. The stars are in place. I am the Zodiac Girl . . ."

Ruth shook her head. "I think you've gone crazy."

"No. Ruth, this is why I *am* the Lady of the Beasts. Don't you see? *Everything* has been leading up to it. I am *supposed* to make this happen. To make other people happy through Bertie. Like Joan of Arc. And Madame Curie. They were both Zodiac Girls, too. I am supposed to comfort the old by taking animals to visit them."

Ruth was still looking at me as though I'd grown an extra head. "But Madame Curie discovered radioactive elements, and Joan of Arc led France into battle against the English. And then she was found guilty of witchcraft and burned at the stake."

"Oh . . . was she? Hmm. Hermie didn't mention that part. But he *did* say that Zodiac Girls all have a different calling. And I'm sure that this is mine. Don't worry. No one's going to burn *me* at the stake for this."

Ruth raised an eyebrow, like she thought that was *exactly* what was going to happen.

Getting rid of Dad was as easy as pie since he was eager to leave to fix the broken-down car. After making me promise to search high and low for Bertie, he said that he'd be back later to pick him up. Then he sped off in his trusty old van.

And now it's time for me to do my rescue job, I thought as energy surged through me. I felt like someone had recharged my flat battery. Plugged me into an electricity source. *Be the fighter you are*, Hermie had said. I would. I felt invincible. I would heal the sick, comfort the old, entertain orphaned children, save the whales . . . Everyone would love Bertie. I'd be a hero and everyone would be happy and both of us would be so popular.

I snuck some pastries up to the room, and Bertie wolfed them down in one gulp. Then we waited until it was time to go and visit the home.

"How are you going to get him out?" asked Ruth. "Someone's bound to notice you. Did any other parents bring pets?"

"Ah, no," I said. "But it won't be a problem. I'll put him in my little wheeled suitcase. But other pets. Hey, good idea, Ruth. Next week, I'll put up a notice inviting the other girls to bring their animals, and we can take a whole bunch down. By then, everyone will have seen how it works, so Chiron House will welcome them all."

"Noooo," Ruth wailed. "Gemma, please. Just get today over with."

I saw her point. Maybe it was a little bit overambitious

to take more than one dog on the first few visits. But I had visions of the future. I would develop my animal-therapy program so that there would be girls going into nursing homes all over the place, all over the country, all over the world, with their pets.

At two o'clock, Ruth began to get her things ready to go to Chiron House.

"I'll see you there," I said as I petted Bertie's head. "I'll wheel him down. It's only five or ten minutes down the driveway. Tell Mrs. Blain that I'm walking down a little bit late."

"Will she allow you on your own?"

"Course. Look, if you're worried, tell her that I was seeing Dad off. She'll understand when I explain later."

"Okay. But I hope you won't get expelled or anything," she said in her usual worried way.

"Not likely," I said. She really didn't see. I'd probably get a medal or an article written about me in the paper. *Lady of the Beasts alive and well and living locally.* Then a TV station would pick it up, and I'd be interviewed for the news. And then I'd be a celebrity and . . . and maybe even be taken to Washington to meet the president! I felt amazing, better than I had in weeks.

After Ruth had left, I waited in the room for ten minutes and then went down to check that everyone who was going to the home had left and that most of the others had gone to the *Bugsy* rehearsals.

Once I was certain that they had, I went back up to get Bertie.

I pulled my suitcase off the top of the bureau, put it on the floor, and unzipped it.

"In," I commanded as I pointed at the case.

Bertie wagged his tail and jumped on the bed.

"*In,*" I said again while still pointing at the case.

Bertie didn't move, except for his wagging tail.

I lifted him off the bed and attempted to put him in the case. Sadly, he thought it was a game, and as soon as I let go, he leaped back on the bed.

I tried again.

"In the case," I said as he tried to lick my face. "In the case."

"Woof," he said and jumped out and then went and hid under the bed, with his nose sticking out from behind the bedspread.

"This isn't a game, Bertie," I said.

"Woof," he said again.

I tried to drag him out, but he wasn't interested and dug his front paws into the carpet.

"I know what will get you out," I said and went to my drawer to find a treat. I got a sugar cookie and held it out to him.

Bertie was out like a shot and gulped it down. Then

I grabbed him and stuffed him inside the suitcase. *Almost there*, I thought as I began to zip him in. I almost had it done when I realized that his right leg was still out. I let go of his front paws and put his right leg in the case. He stuck the left leg out.

"Bertie!" I cried in exasperation. "Just get in the case."

He looked at me quizzically and licked my hand. I grabbed the stray leg with one hand and then quickly zipped up the case around him with the other hand.

He gave me one of Ruth's "what-on-earth-are-you-doing-now?" looks as his face disappeared into the case. I left a few inches open so that he could breathe, and, quick as a flash, he'd stuck a paw through and was trying to open it.

"Stay *still*, Bertie," I said as I stuffed his paw back down.

He let out a soft whine and then, at last, seemed to settle in the case.

I opened the door and looked left and then right down the corridor. All clear. I headed for the stairs. I couldn't wheel the case down the stairs, so I lifted it up and staggered down. It was really heavy. Inside the case, Bertie had begun struggling again, and his nose was poking out of the opening.

"Stay *in*," I urged him, praying that no one would come out and see me. Luckily, no one did, so I made it to the bottom of the stairs and then dashed for the front door.

Outside at the front, I put down the case. *So far, so good*, I thought as I hurriedly began wheeling it down the driveway, trying to look as cool as I could. I'd just reached the end of the courtyard when I heard a voice.

"Whiting!"

I turned to see Dr. Cronus coming after me.

"And where do you think you're going?" he asked, looking at my case. "Not running away, are we?"

We, running away? *We? Omigod. Does he know that Bertie's in the case?* For a moment I panicked and then realized that "we" was just a figure of speech. He meant was *I* running away.

"No, sir. Outreach program, sir," I said. "Mrs. Blain asked me to take some books down to Chiron House, and they were heavy, so I thought I'd wheel them there."

Dr. Cronus narrowed his eyes and scrutinized me closely. I held my breath and hoped that Bertie was doing the same.

"Off you go, then," said Dr. Cronus, and he turned to go back to the school.

As I began to walk away, Bertie let out a soft bark, as if to say, *Hey, I'm still in here.* I began to fake a coughing fit as Dr. Cronus turned back.

"Hay fever, sir," I said.

"In September?"

"It's the eucalyptus, sir. It gets me every time."

Dr. Cronus rolled his eyes. "See the nurse when you get back."

"Yes, sir, Dr. Cronus, sir," I said, and then I legged it as fast as I could down the driveway.

Halfway there, the case began to feel really heavy, even though it was on wheels. The distance from the bottom of the driveway to Chiron House took a couple of minutes in the car, but by foot it was another matter. As soon as we were around a corner and out of sight of the school, I unzipped the case, let Bertie out, and put him on his leash.

He was delighted to be out in the open and began to run ahead, dragging me with him. I did my best to keep up with him, but he was too strong for me and pulled the leash out of my hand. He raced off down the driveway and around the next corner. I chased after him, but as I turned the corner, there was no sign of him.

"Oh, *no*," I cried. "*Bertie*. Bad dog. Heel."

Only silence greeted me.

Fifty yards away, I could see Chiron House.

Oh, bummer, I thought. *Now what? Now I really* have *lost Bertie. Dad's going to kill me when he gets back.*

I stood on the driveway, not knowing which way to turn. Whether to go back, forward, or just lie down and cry.

Dad was right. Darned dog. How could I ever have thought that Bertie could comfort the old when he drove the young completely and totally crazy?

"BERTIE!!!"

Chapter Fourteen

Oops!

I started to walk back to the school. *Best just go and wait for Dad and tell the truth*, I thought. *No point in going on to Chiron House now. I'd never be able to concentrate.* I felt completely defeated.

As I made my way back up the driveway, I suddenly heard a familiar roar. Hermie!

I turned around to see the most amazing sight. Hermie was riding toward me on his motorcycle, and sitting in front of him, paws up on the handlebars and ears blown back, was Bertie. I burst out laughing. They looked so ridiculous.

Hermie pulled up beside me.

"Lose someone?" he asked.

I nodded. "He pulled the leash out of my hand," I said. "Thanks so much for bringing him back. Bad dog, Bertie."

Bertie turned and gave Hermie a lick.

Hermie grinned and scratched Bertie's ear. "He's very sorry, aren't you, boy? I found him out on the road. He seemed to enjoy the ride."

Bertie raised an ear and barked in agreement.

"But how did you know that he was mine?"

Hermie turned his bike around. "He told me, of course," he said. Bertie woofed in agreement and then gave Hermie a last lick and jumped off the bike. "Catch you both later." And he blasted off down the driveway.

"So now he can communicate with animals as well as everyone else?" I said to Bertie as I held onto his leash for dear life and then turned to Chiron House. All was not lost. Once again, my hero, Hermie, had appeared out of the blue to come to my rescue.

When we reached Chiron House, I knocked on the door and waited a few minutes, but no one answered, so I tried the huge brass doorknob to see if it was open. It was, and Bertie and I slipped in. At the reception desk was a girl who looked only a few years older than me. She was sitting with her feet up on the desk, her eyes closed, and a set of headphones on, so she didn't hear us until we were almost on top of her. When she realized that someone was there, she just about leaped out of her skin.

"Omigod!" she exclaimed as she removed the headphones. "You shouldn't sneak up on people like that."

"Oh. Sorry . . . didn't mean to startle you . . ."

"So? Waddayawant?"

I made myself stand up tall and look confident.

"I'm with the . . . um . . . the animal-comfort-for-the-elderly program. I . . . I haven't seen you here before?"

"Yeah. So?" said the girl with a shrug. "I'm standing in for my mom while she's out shopping. I think some of your group have gone in already." She jerked her thumb down a corridor. "Down there. With all the wrinklies."

Phew, I thought. *That was lucky.* I had my story about animal therapy all straight in my head, but I was glad that it had been her at the desk and not Nurse Stepford.

I led Bertie in the direction that she'd pointed, and there, through glass-paneled double-swing doors, I could see the ladies having tea and sandwiches. A few of the girls from our school were talking or reading to their ladies, and Ruth was walking around with a tray of teacups.

"Okay, Bertie, destiny awaits," I said as I patted his head and took a deep breath. "It's showtime, folks."

I opened the door and walked in.

"WAGGGGGGGHHHHHHHH!" shrieked Mrs. Compton-Grime, her eyes popping out farther than usual the moment she spotted Bertie. "NURSE!" she screeched as she cowered back in her chair. "It's a dog, a nasty, *filthy* dog. Get him out of here. Get HIM OUT OF HERE!"

Another one of the ladies dropped her teacup, while the others stared in amazement as Bertie, being the friendly soul that he is, raced over and bounded onto Mrs. Compton-Grime's lap, where he started furiously licking her face.

"ARRRGGH SPPLUURGGGG YUCCCKKK," she shouted as she tried to push him off.

Unfortunately, Bertie thought that she was playing a game and licked all the harder.

"Smmurffffgruumphhh, off, get *off*," she blustered and finally pushed Bertie off her lap. Suddenly airborne, Bertie managed a quick twist and landed with a soft thump on her knitting basket, knocking it over and creating a multicolored torrent of woolen yarn as balls rolled off in all directions.

Oh, bummer, I thought as he dived after them. He loves balls of yarn—he used to play with them when he was a puppy.

"Not my knitting, *not my knitting*, off, *off*, OFF!" cried Mrs. Compton-Grime, desperately grabbing at a ball of her yarn.

Bertie immediately took this as a sign that another game had begun and tried to pull it out of her hand with his teeth.

I rushed over to try to get him away, but he was off, the ball of yarn firmly clamped in his mouth.

"*No*. STOOOPPP him!" screeched Mrs Compton-Grime as she tried to grasp the four-legged rocket, but he was too fast for her and dived under a low table that had been set for tea. The cups rattled in their saucers and the tea slopped a bit, but mercifully the cups stayed upright.

From there, Bertie skidded around another chair and over a sofa. Then he repeated the action in reverse. By now, all of the girls were chasing him. A jumping, diving, slipping, sliding, laughing mob frantically followed the trail of bright red yarn that now covered half the room. The old ladies watched in horrified silence as their tranquil parlor turned into mayhem, and at the center of the chaos sat Mrs. Compton-Grime. Around and around and around her chair ran Bertie, until yards of yarn were wrapped around her. Trapped by the yarn, she was a prisoner in her own chair and screamed to the high heavens for Nurse Stepford.

"NUUUUUUUUUURSE!"

"Sorry," I said as I made a dive for Bertie. "Oh, I'm so, *so* sorry."

Suddenly the ball of yarn ran out, and Bertie stopped dead in his tracks—as did his throng of pursuers, who collided with each other and ended up in a messy pile of arms and legs at Mrs. Compton-Grime's feet.

For a second or two, there was silence.

Disappointed by the red ball's disappearance, an out-of-breath Bertie flopped on his belly, legs splayed out on both sides of him.

It was time to make my move, and I quietly approached him. Slowly, I reached out and was about to grab him, when a cat popped its head out from underneath the sofa. Disturbed from a deep sleep, it had been observing the situation, wisely waiting until the insanity stopped before attempting to escape. Unfortunately, it stepped right in front of Bertie, who perked up immediately. *Oh, no,* I thought, *chasing cats is another one of Bertie's favorite games.*

"Woof. GRRRR. Woof," growled Bertie.

"MEOOWWWWWW," replied the cat.

"Arrrghh," Mrs. Compton-Grime said with a sigh and slumped back into her chair as if someone had let all the air out of her.

The cat stopped, arched its back, and seemed to double in size as every strand of its fur stood on end.

"Bertie, heel, *heel,*" I cried as everyone in the room looked on in anticipation.

But Bertie wasn't listening. He leaped to his feet, and the two stood looking at each other like two gunfighters, eyeball to eyeball, nose to nose. Then the cat made a run for the French doors.

Bertie dashed after it, hitting the low table and sending the teacups, plates, and sandwiches flying.

The cat hit the door. It was closed. Bertie skidded into the cat, who let out a terrible wail and clawed its way up the curtains. To Bertie, this was a fun new twist to the game, so he sank his teeth into the folds of material and began to shake it violently. The cat hung on, digging its claws deeper as the soft velvet spun around and around.

"Maybe we'd better let them out," said Rose, going to the door and unlatching it.

"Noooo," I cried, "not without his leash." But it was too late; she'd done it, and the cat shot off outside. In the few seconds it took for Bertie to realize that his prey was no longer confined to the curtains, the cat had run halfway across the yard. With a bark of enthusiasm, Bertie spotted it, and the chase was on again. Over flower beds and around the rosebushes they raced, both getting muddier and muddier. Then the cat made an almighty leap over the high garden wall, and it was all over.

After a few triumphant barks and a quick scratch, Bertie trotted back over the muddy flower beds and reentered the room, where, blind to the scene of complete devastation surrounding him, he began vacuuming up the sandwiches and cookies that lay scattered all over the floor.

At that moment, Nurse Stepford walked in. "What the . . . ?" she exclaimed after taking in the half-torn-down curtains, the smashed cups and plates, the overturned chairs and tables, and, finally, Mrs.

Compton-Grime, who was still tied to her chair. Nurse Stepford's eyes rolled up into the back of her head, and she fainted.

Oh, nooooooo! I thought. Bertie's *third* favorite game! He loves it when people play dead. He was quick off the mark—in a flash, he was on Nurse Stepford's chest, attempting resuscitation by pawing her and licking her face with great enthusiasm.

It seemed to work.

She slowly opened her eyes to see a large pink tongue covering her face. Behind this she must have seen a small bundle of furry mud, much of which was sticking to her perfect white uniform. She gave a sigh and passed out again.

I pulled Bertie off her as most of the other old ladies, who were clearly anxious about what he was going to do next, cowered behind the sofa. Only Mrs. Hamilton seemed to be unfazed by the scene. In fact, she seemed to be highly amused. I gave her an apologetic look as I picked up Bertie and held him tightly in my arms. He gave my cheek a huge lick, as if to thank me for giving him the time of his life.

"We're leaving, we're leaving," I said in an attempt to reassure the worried ladies. "He's harmless, honestly. He won't hurt anyone."

"WHO is responsible for this?" asked a stern voice behind me.

I turned to see Mrs. Blain, who had just come in from the kitchen carrying a fresh pot of tea.

All eyes turned to me.

What could I possibly say to get out of this? I wondered as her astonished face turned my way.

"Um . . . oops!"

Chapter Fifteen

Suspension?

The Lady of the Beasts is in the doghouse.

It would be funny if everyone wasn't so angry at me.

Dad hit the roof when he got back and found out what I had done. He apologized profusely to everyone and then made a speedy exit, taking Bertie with him.

I called Hermie as soon as I got back to school, but there was no response. In fact, the phone seemed to have gone dead. I tried to check the site, but the computer kept crashing, and when I finally managed to get online, there was nothing there either except a message confirming what Hermie had said in the deli. Mercury has gone retrograde. The one time I really needed him, and he'd done a disappearing act.

Mrs. Blain could hardly speak to me—she was so angry. She'd marched me back up to the school and straight in to see Dr. Cronus.

"What on earth did you think you were doing?" he asked when she'd explained the situation.

"I was trying to help, sir. I thought that some of the

old people might like to see a nice pet."

Mrs. Blain clicked her tongue at the mention of the words "nice pet."

"A *nice* pet?" she said. "Is that what you call him? Do you call what he got up to the behavior of a nice pet? More like a wild beast. The ladies were very upset, and Mrs. Compton-Grime looked like she was going to have a heart attack. Not to mention Nurse Stepford. She had to go home to rest. And after all our good work there, now they've threatened to ban us."

Dr. Cronus's eyes were boring into me. "Do you realize how this reflects on Avebury, Whiting?"

"Yes, sir. Sorry, sir. I didn't mean to upset anyone. I really . . . I'm sorry."

"I should think so. Taking a wild dog into a nursing home? You must be insane. There are organized programs for that sort of thing. Programs where the animals are *trained*."

There was nothing more I could say in my defense, so I hung my head, stared at the floor, and waited to hear my punishment.

Of course, news of my exploits was all around the school by Monday morning.

"What happened?" asked Rose Watson at breakfast. "We thought you'd been expelled when you didn't come down last night."

"I was sent to bed early without any dinner," I said. "Dr. Cronus said I had to reflect on my actions."

Sara and crew suddenly appeared at the end of the table.

"So, are you going to get expelled?" asked Sara.

I bet she'd love that, I thought as I took a halfhearted bite of my toast.

"Leave her alone," said Ruth. "Can't you see that she's been through enough?"

"Oh, the mouse speaks . . . or squeaks," Sara said with a laugh, but she did back off.

Tasha, however, lingered behind and sat down across from me.

Ruth gave her a hard stare as if to say, *Get lost.* Tasha leaned over and touched my wrist.

"I'm not going to make fun of you," she said. "I just wondered what happened. Are they going to expel you?"

I shook my head. "Don't think so. Dr. Cronus did say that I came close to it, but since I'm a new girl and it was my first offense, I'm likely to just get suspended for a week. The teachers are going to discuss my case on Friday, and that's when I'll hear. In the meantime, I've been forbidden to go within a hundred yards of Chiron House, or I'll be expelled."

"Suspension," said Tasha. "That could be cool. It would mean a week at home!"

I shook my head again. Even though a week ago I couldn't wait to get home, I realized that it was the last thing I needed right now, not under these circumstances. A week out, and I'd get behind with schoolwork—and I'd never fit in or find friends.

"My parents will kill me. I'll never hear the end of it. And in the meantime I have to stay in my room every night, and I'm not allowed into the common room. I didn't mean to cause any trouble. I thought that it must be so boring sitting in that nursing home all day long, and seeing a pet might cheer them up. Bertie's usually so well behaved."

At the table at the far end of the room, Sara, Mercedes, and Lois were glaring angrily. Not only at me, but also at Tasha.

"Won't your friends be missing you?" asked Ruth.

Tasha shook her head. "Don't care," she said, and then she smiled kindly. "I wanted to check that you were okay. And . . . and I wanted to say that I'm sorry that we . . . *I've* been mean to you. You didn't deserve it."

I felt my eyes fill with sudden tears. I put my hands up to my face so that no one could see. "Don't be nice to me . . . You'll . . . you'll . . . make me cry."

Tasha laughed. "I thought I made you cry by *not* being nice to you."

I laughed, and Tasha smiled again.

"Do you think, maybe . . . well, maybe we could be

friends?" she asked.

"But Sara and Mercedes . . . ?"

Tasha glanced over at them and then made a face. "Between you and me, they're not much fun. All they ever seem to do is talk about other people and be horrible to them. It can get a little bit tiring, being around people who are so negative all the time. I thought from day one when we saw you coming out of that storage closet that

you looked like fun, and I felt really mean when they didn't invite you or Ruth to the late-night party. Up until now, I guess I felt scared of them, in a way. Like if I went against them, they'd gang up on me, too. But now I don't care. After I saw you stand up to Sara that time outside, I realized that I was being cowardly and it was time that I stood up to them as well."

"Good for you," said Ruth, who was beginning to speak out more and more herself.

"Tell us the part where Bertie tied Mrs. Compton-Grime up with her knitting again," said Imogen, coming over from the next table to join us.

The image of Bertie and the yarn did make me smile for a moment, although it hadn't seemed funny at the time.

"And the old biddy was okay, you know," said Rose. "As soon as you'd left, she sat up, as right as rain. I think she's an old drama queen who likes to cause trouble."

"That's probably how Sara and her friends will end up," said Tasha. "Bitter old ladies in a nursing home with nothing better to do than grumble and make other people's lives miserable."

"Bertie really misbehaved, though," I said.

"I guess," said Rose, "but there was no lasting damage done, and Mrs. Hamilton said that she hadn't had such a good laugh in years and we should all go back as soon as possible."

"Really?" I said. I couldn't believe my ears. Last night, I thought my life was over. The old ladies hated me. The teachers were mad at me. No one at school liked me except for Ruth, and yet here I was, surrounded by friendly faces, having breakfast and laughing. *Exactly how I'd hoped it would be*, I thought.

On Tuesday evening, Rose and Imogen invited Ruth and me to a sleepover in their room. Everyone wanted to hear the story of Bertie's visit over and over again. Even some of the juniors and seniors stopped by for a while to sympathize.

"Tough," said Fleur. "Okay, you acted irresponsibly, but you don't deserve to be suspended. Everyone makes mistakes."

On the website, there was still zilch. On the phone,

also zilch.

Where are you, Hermie? I wondered as the week went on.

By Friday, I was starting to get seriously worried about my future. Even though I'd been on my best behavior all week and had done as I was told, the teachers were distant with me, and Mrs. Blain, who was usually so friendly, treated me like an outcast.

On Friday afternoon, half of our class went off to the rehearsal for *Bugsy* as usual, and Ruth was preparing to go to the outreach program meeting.

"Are you sure you can't come?" Ruth asked.

I shook my head. "My case comes up this afternoon, so Mrs. Blain said to sit this one out until the school has decided what to do with me. As a punishment, she's given me sentences to write. What are you going to do at the meeting, now that Chiron House has threatened to ban us?"

"I guess we're going to have to make new plans and find new places to go," said Ruth.

"That's not fair," I said. "I feel so bad, because it wasn't anybody else's fault. I caused the trouble. I feel rotten, especially because I think that Mrs. Hamilton looked forward to us going."

"I know," said Ruth. "I liked her, but it seems like Mrs. Compton-Grime calls the shots around there."

After Ruth had gone to the meeting, I sat down and began writing my sentences.

I will not take pets into nursing homes.

I will not take pets into nursing homes.

I will not take pets into nursing homes.

I wrote the sentence over and over. By the hundredth sentence, I was getting bored. I checked my phone, but there was still no message from Hermie, so I went to the astrology site.

There were five messages.

Sorry that I haven't been in touch, but I've been feeling a bit backward lately.

Wrongs can be made right.

Nothing is over until it's over.

Keep fighting.

Listen to your inner voice.

Back soon. Hermie

What inner voice? I asked myself. *Isn't listening to inner voices what crazy people do?* I decided that I was a bit crazy, so why not give it a try? I sat quietly to try and tune in to my inner voice. At first I felt stupid as various thoughts floated through my head.

I wonder what's for dinner tonight.

I wonder if I will be suspended and what I'll say to Mom and Dad. And Grandma?

It'd be nice to see Jess and the girls, though.

But they'll all be at school, so most of the time I'd be

by myself.

Keep fighting. How?

And then it seemed like the floodgates had opened, and my inner Gemini twins were having an argument.

Life is what I make of it. A disaster so far.

Stay in and write my sentences.

Be myself. I'm a fighter.

No, I'm not. I don't want to cause trouble.

Nothing is over until it's over.

I am the Lady of the Beasts. Grrrr.

I am the Zodiac Girl. Arghhh.

What should I do?

Stay in my room and lie low.

Go to Chiron House and apologize.

But I'll get expelled.

Go to Chiron House and apologize.

But I'll get into trouble.

Go to Chiron House and apologize.

Go to Chiron House and apologize.

Go to Chiron House and apologize.

Go to Chiron House and apologize.

Go to Chiron House and apologize.

Go to Chiron House and apologize.

It seemed like my split personality had merged, and the Gemini twins that live in my head agreed on something at last. Either that, or one of them had punched the other's lights out.

I had to go to Chiron House and apologize.

I tried to call Hermie and ask what he thought, but the line was still dead, so I pulled my jacket out of the closet and put on my black woolly hat. I figured that if I pulled the hat down over my head until I got to the nursing home, any teachers who might see me sneaking off wouldn't realize that it was me.

I didn't see anyone when I got downstairs, so I made for the front door and then ran as fast as I could down the driveway.

I got within a few yards of Chiron House, and then panic hit me. What was I doing? Dr. Cronus had said that I'd be expelled if I went within a hundred yards of Chiron House, and here I was, right outside. Did I really want to be expelled? A week ago, it would have been the answer to all of my problems. I'd be back with my old friends. I'd be back at home. But now I didn't want it to happen that way.

I was about to set off back up the driveway when I saw someone coming from the back of Chiron House.

"WHO'S THERE?" croaked an elderly voice.

I ducked down behind the bushes, hoping that I could still get away. I heard the sound of footsteps shuffling behind me, and before I knew it, someone had poked me hard in the back with a cane.

"OW!" I cried before I could stop myself.

"Come out of that bush, whoever you are," commanded the voice. "Stand up and show yourself."

Slowly, I crawled out and reluctantly stood up, to see Mrs. Compton-Grime's angry face staring at me over the hedge.

"You! What on earth are you doing there?" she demanded. "Explain yourself."

"I . . . I came to apologize," I stuttered.

"Apologize! Herumph," she said with a sniff. "Bit late for that. I thought I'd told them not to let you come within a hundred yards of this place."

"I . . . I know . . . I just . . ."

"No 'just' about it, missy. Clearly you don't know how to follow rules. Now, off with you. Out of here. And I can tell you, the school will be hearing from me very soon about this matter."

Chapter Sixteen

Bummer

Idiot, idiot, idiot, I said to myself over and over again as I made my way back up to the school. *Why did I listen to my inner voice? Why did I listen to Hermie? He's only gotten me into deeper and deeper trouble since day one. I wish I'd never met him. I wish I'd never found out about that stupid site. I wish I weren't a Zodiac Girl. Now I am going to get expelled.*

As the school came into view, I saw Ruth at the window in the dining room. She waved excitedly when she saw me and then disappeared, only to reappear at the door a few moments later.

"Where have you been?" she asked breathlessly as I got closer. "We've been looking for you everywhere. You won't believe what's happened. Quick, come into the annex."

"Why? What is it?" I asked. "Has someone heard about my punishment?"

"No, nothing like that," said Ruth as she led me to the annex. "Come to the outreach meeting. You'll soon see."

As we got closer to the annex, I could hear shouting. Mostly from Mrs. Blain.

I opened the door and could hardly believe what I saw. It was complete pandemonium. A zoo where all of the animals had run wild. And poor Mrs. Blain in the middle of it all, looking like she was living her worst nightmare.

Rose was there with Boris the cat, who was desperately trying to escape up one of the wooden blinds on the window, swinging by one paw.

Imogen was holding on to one of the school goats. He was chewing his way through a pile of papers on a teacher's desk.

Grace was busy chasing a couple of hens, who were clucking like crazy, trying to find an exit, and one of them pooped close to Mrs. Blain's feet.

Alice Jacobs had a cage containing the mice from the science lab, and next to her was Marie Wilkinson with a box of frogs, also from the science lab. They gave me the thumbs-up and cheered loudly when they saw me appear at the door.

Hannah Morrison came rushing over, carrying a fishbowl. "I've brought a tadpole," she said. "Um. They don't do much unless you swish the water around."

"And I've brought my imaginary pet," said Lucia Peters with a grin. "There wasn't anything left by the time I heard about it, so I had to be creative."

"Heard about what?" I asked. I was mystified. What on earth was going on?

Ruth squeezed my arm. "Revolution," she said. "The girls are revolting."

"Well, that's a bit harsh," I said. "I know we didn't like a lot of them in the beginning, but I wouldn't go that far."

"Girls, GIRLS," bellowed Mrs. Blain above the din. "SETTLE DOWN."

The girls became quieter, but the animals continued squawking and meowing and bleating.

"Okay," said Mrs. Blain above the cacophony. "Who's going to explain this extraordinary display of . . . of . . . *outrageous* behavior?"

Ruth giggled. "It was Tasha's idea," she whispered to me. "She said we had to do something to help you."

"Is SOMEBODY going to tell me what's going on?" demanded Mrs. Blain.

Tasha motioned for Ruth to speak up. Ruth turned bright red and took a deep breath. "If Gemma gets suspended," she said, "we all get suspended. We've all brought animals for the animal-therapy program, so Gemma's not the only one."

"Yes," said Tasha. "If Gemma goes, we all go!"

My jaw fell open.

So did Mrs. Blain's.

So did the goat's. But for a different reason. I don't

think he liked the taste of the books, and he looked like he was going to throw up.

A dark shadow appeared at the door, and I turned to see Dr. Cronus standing there, taking in the scene in front of him. He had a face like thunder as he looked around.

"If Gemma gets suspended, we all do," said Ruth again, but this time it came out as barely a whisper.

"All of you," said Dr. Cronus after a few moments. "In your rooms, NOW. And I don't want to see one of your faces until we have decided your fate."

Oh, God, I thought as I trooped out with the others. If I wasn't up for expulsion when Mrs. Compton-Grime had her say, I certainly was after this little episode.

"I'm not sorry," said Ruth later as we sat on the windowsill of our room and stared out at the trees. "I'd do it again if we had the chance."

"Thanks, Ruth," I said, "but I don't want to get you in trouble for something that was my fault. Or the others. I'm going to take the blame."

Ruth laughed. "It was funny, wasn't it? Did you see that hen poop near Mrs.—"

"Omigod. Quick, down," I said as I leaped off the sill and pulled Ruth with me.

"What? What?" she said as she fell onto the floor. "What did you see?"

"Car," I said as I knelt up and peeked to see out the window.

Ruth knelt up beside me. "What car? Who?"

I pointed down into the courtyard, where an old Rolls Royce had just pulled up. In the backseat, I could clearly see Nurse Stepford's white uniform and the shape of someone next to her, someone with white hair. Ruth knelt up a little bit higher as I quickly filled her in on my attempted visit to Chiron House.

"Oh, God," she said. "That's done it."

I ducked down further. "I don't want them to see me. That has to be Mrs. Compton-Grime with Nurse Stepford. What can you see?"

"It *is* Nurse Stepford," she said. "Definitely. She's getting out and going around to the other door. She's helping someone out . . . one of the old ladies, I can't see . . ." She quickly ducked down again. "Nurse Stepford looked up at the windows."

"It has to be Mrs. Compton-Grime with her," I said with a sigh. "Come to demand that they take me out. She said she would. And if she is the school's benefactor, it's all over for me."

Ruth peeked. "I can't see," she said. "They're going toward Dr. Cronus's office. I can only see their backs . . . oh . . . but . . . oh, I am sorry, Gemma."

I rolled over and lay on the carpet. "Bummer," I said. "That's definitely me finished."

Chapter Seventeen

Surprise visitor

"Might as well pack my bags, then," I said gloomily as I pulled my case down from the top of the bureau.

Ruth sat on the end of her bed and kept offering me chocolate. I didn't have the appetite for it, though. I had a sick feeling in my stomach as I imagined Mom and Dad's disappointment when they heard the news. I felt so guilty. All of the hours they'd spent working so that they could give me this opportunity, and now it was like throwing it back in their faces. They were bound to think that I'd done it on purpose.

When I was almost done packing, I sat on the foot of the bed, ready to hear my fate.

"I'll really, really miss you," said Ruth.

"Me, too," I said and then attempted to give her a smile. "In fact, I'll be sorry to leave . . ."

"Check the astrology site. See if Hermie has anything to say."

I shook my head and lay back on the bed. "It's all too late."

But Ruth went to the desk anyway, turned on the

computer, and this time it didn't crash as she typed in the site address.

Just as it was downloading, we heard a gentle tap on the door.

Ruth got up to open the door. She looked surprised. "Oh. Hi," she said. "Um . . ."

"Well? Can I come in?" asked a familiar voice.

"Yes, of course, come in. Gemma, look who it is," said Ruth as Mrs. Hamilton stepped in and looked around.

She glanced at me and then went over to the window. "Ah," she said. "This brings back memories." Then she saw my suitcase on the floor. "Wherever are you going, child?"

I looked at the floor. "Home, I guess. Expelled."

"*Expelled?* Whatever makes you say that?"

"Mrs. Compton-Grime. I think she's in with Dr. Cronus now . . ."

Mrs. Hamilton sat on the bed and motioned for me to sit up next to her. "Tell me everything," she said as she patted my hand.

She listened patiently as I told her my whole crazy, sad story.

". . . so you see, they're bound to ask me to leave." I sighed as I finished.

"Nonsense," she said.

"*Nonsense?* How can you say that? After what I've done . . ."

Mrs. Hamilton smiled. "Nothing compared with what I got up to when I was here!"

"But . . . I saw Mrs. Compton-Grime arrive with Nurse Stepford. And . . . and I think she's a benefactor of our school, and what she says goes . . . and she said . . . What? You were a student here?"

"I was," Mrs. Hamilton said and smiled. "And never mind what Mrs. Compton-Grime said. It was me who arrived just now with Nurse Stepford. And it's *me* who's the school's benefactor. Mrs. Compton-Grime hasn't got two pennies to rub together. She just likes to pretend that she's very grand."

"So . . . so . . . what's going to happen . . . ?"

But Mrs. Hamilton was up again. She'd seen the website on my computer and sat at the desk.

"What's all this?" she asked.

"Ah . . ." I said. That was the part I'd omitted from the story. "It's . . . um . . . it's an . . ."

"An astrology site," said Ruth.

Mrs. Hamilton stared at the screen for a few moments and then at me in amazement. "You're a Zodiac Girl? You *are*, aren't you?" She looked back at the screen. "Oh, this explains everything! Oh, this is *marvelous*. In my day, I got my messages in the mail, and what a slow process it was. But *this*, of *course*, the Internet . . ."

"In your day?" I asked. "What do you mean? How

did you know that I was a Zodiac Girl?"

She pulled out a necklace from underneath her blouse. It was a tiny silver zodiac symbol on a chain, similar to mine. "Because I was one!" She grinned as she showed us her necklace. "The Water Bearer, see? I'm an Aquarius, so that's my symbol. *I* was a Zodiac Girl. Oh, this is too wonderful. I've never met another one before. I knew that there were others out there, but I never knew when or where."

I nodded. "But . . . how . . . ?"

Mrs. Hamilton shrugged. "Been going on for centuries apparently . . ."

"I know. Joan of Arc. Madam Curie," I said.

"Yes. I was told that. But they managed to do more . . . um . . . good than I did. So. Who's your guardian?"

"I'm a Gemini, so it's a motorcycle messenger guy named Hermie. Hermie for Hermes, for Mercury. He's Dr. Cronus's grandson."

Mrs. Hamilton shook her head. "Hermie? The gorgeous *Hermie?* No. It's not possible. He used to bring the mail up on his bicycle when I was here. He was oh, around nineteen, maybe twenty, looked like a Greek god. We all had the biggest crushes on him, all of us vying for his attention and trying to get him to give us a ride on his bike. Sadly, I never won. Ah, but he must be ancient by now. Well, older than me."

"No. No," said Ruth. "He still looks about twenty.

I wonder if he's the same person?"

"I bet he is," I said. "Or the same being." I looked at Mrs. Hamilton. "You must have seen him whizzing up and down on his motorcycle."

She shook her head. "No. No, I haven't. But, then, so many people pass us by at Chiron House, as if we're invisible in there. Then again, as you know, I haven't been there long. I used to live in my own house until . . . well, until it became clear that I couldn't manage it anymore."

"We think that Dr. Cronus may be Saturn. I don't suppose he was here in your day," said Ruth.

Mrs. Hamilton nodded. "Oh, yes. Old Cronus we used to call him. He was here, all right. I've just been in having a chat with him. He looked old back when I was in school. I just thought he was one of those people who always looked ancient. And he still does. I didn't know that he was Hermie's grandfather, though. Well, I never!" She clapped her hands. "But this is too exciting! Another Zodiac Girl. No wonder so much has been going on! I didn't know what had hit me when it was my time. It changed my whole life, and I'll certainly never forget it." Then she laughed. "And they will *certainly* never forget me."

"Why? What happened?" asked Ruth.

Mrs. Hamilton smiled mischievously. "I burned down the science lab. Didn't mean to. Of course I didn't. It was Uri. He was my guardian. Uri for Uranus. He rules Aquarius. I was a very shy child. Timid as a mouse. He told me that I had to experiment. I realized later that he meant in life—not in the chemistry lab!"

Ruth and I gasped.

"Yes," continued Mrs. Hamilton. "Uranus brings the unexpected. It's symbolized by a bolt of lightning sometimes. Tee-hee. What I did was certainly unexpected. Mixed a few chemicals together in the spirit of discovery and trying to do what Uri had instructed me to, when kebang, blast, and kerpow. No more science lab. Luckily, no one was hurt, but I was expelled and sent to school in Switzerland. Uri told me that I was supposed to make a difference, and I did! Not in the way I expected, though. That's why, later in life, I became a benefactor of the school. I wanted to make up for my . . . um . . . somewhat explosive time here."

Ruth and I both laughed.

"So, Gemma Whiting," continued Mrs. Hamilton, "all I can say is, don't you worry. It took me a while, but I made it right in the end. *Am* making it right. This school would have closed long ago without my help. Sometimes it's a mystery in life, but good can come from disaster. If I hadn't felt indebted to the school, I would never have felt the need to help keep it going."

"So you think I might get expelled, and maybe later, when I'm rich or famous, I'll come back and give them some money?"

Mrs. Hamilton burst out laughing. "Oh, no. Nothing like that. We all have our individual paths to walk. No. With you, I don't think it's going to take quite so long to find your calling."

She had a mischievous glint in her eyes again. *Oh, dear*, I thought. *She blew up the science lab. What on earth does she think I'll end up doing?*

Chapter Eighteen

Awards

It was the evening before the last day of the term, and everyone was ready for the performance of *Bugsy*. The school had been decorated for Christmas. A tall tree covered in red bows and balls stood in the hall, and the corridors were covered with ivy, holly, and tinsel. Some of the juniors and seniors had made decorations out of cinnamon sticks, cloves, and orange peels and had hung them from the ceiling so that everywhere smelled good as well as looked festive.

The show was due to start at 7:30 P.M., but everyone—students, parents, and guests alike—had been asked to be in their seats in the assembly hall at 7:00 P.M. for a short awards ceremony.

"Well, we made it to the end of the term," I said to Ruth as we filed in and took the seats that Tasha had saved for us on the left-hand side of the hall.

"Yeah, phew!" she said. "And you were so sure that old Cronus was going to expel you. That time seems like ages ago now."

"I know. You know what was weird, though? He

never said anything more about it."

"Maybe Mrs. Hamilton put in a good word for you," suggested Ruth.

"Maybe. But even if she did, I can't believe that Cronus would listen. You know what he's like. Maybe he thought he'd let me see out the rest of the year, and then it will be like, Merry Christmas, oh, and by the way, you're expelled."

"No way. Surely he wouldn't be that mean," said Ruth as she waved to my mom and dad, who were seated halfway back on the guest side of the hall. She'd become good friends with them since the beginning of the term, plus she was going to be spending Christmas vacation with us since her parents were still overseas and her alternative would have been staying at the school with Dr. Cronus and the other students who had parents who were out of the country. In the row behind Mom and Dad, Hermie was seated with Nessa and Joe. Hermie saw me and gave me the thumbs-up.

"Have you seen Sara preening herself?" asked Ruth as she glanced over at the cast from the show, who were seated in the front of the hall so that they could get backstage quickly when the prize giving was over. "She's probably hoping for one of the awards tonight, but there are only three to be given out, according to Mrs. Blain, so she'd be lucky if she got one."

I glanced over to where Ruth had been looking. It was the first time that all of the cast had been in full costume. Even though there had been a dress rehearsal the week before, Mrs. Woods had a superstition about not wearing costumes until the night of the show and so wouldn't let anyone get into their outfits until tonight, in case anything happened. They looked great, Sara in particular, and I couldn't help but feel a stab of envy. She had her hair slicked back into a bun at the back of her head and had pulled a curl out over her forehead just like Jodie Foster had done in the movie. She was wearing full makeup, a gorgeous gray silk slip of a dress, and, around her neck, she had on a baby pink feather boa. She saw me looking at her, blew me a kiss, and gave me a fake smile. I smiled back. I didn't care anymore about her horrible treatment. I had real friends now, and that was what mattered.

Dr. Cronus got up onto the stage, and the hall grew quiet in anticipation.

"I'd like to welcome everyone," said Dr. Cronus as he looked out at the rows of people in front of him. "I'm so happy to see that so many of you have turned out for our show, and so I won't keep you for long. I'd just like to say that we're very lucky to have a most esteemed guest with us this evening. She's been a tremendous support to our school both in the past and in the present, so I'd like you all to give a very warm welcome to the honorable Mrs. Hamilton."

I almost got the giggles, as Dr. Cronus giving anyone a warm *anything* was a stretch of the imagination—as was the idea of him being happy to see everyone there. He looked his usual glum self as he stood there on the stage.

A moment later, Fleur was seen helping Mrs. Hamilton up the stairs to join the headmaster.

Mrs. Hamilton stood at the podium and looked around. "Good evening," she said. "As an old student of the school, I can't tell you what a great pleasure it is to be here. It always brings back many happy memories and many . . . many . . . um . . . should I say, not-so-happy ones. School days can be a roller coaster for all of us. Good times, bad times. But I'm not here to bore you with my reminiscences. I'm not here to talk about the past. I'm here to talk about the future. As you know, there have been various projects happening around the school to raise funds. The school play . . ."

At this point, I saw Sara sit up a little straighter as though she was waiting for an acknowledgment. She also reached up to her neck, gave it a good scratch, and a bit of her hair came out of its clip at the back.

Ruth must have noticed, too, because she nudged me. "Looks like Sara's feather boa might have fleas," she said and giggled. "She's been scratching herself since she sat down."

". . . I look forward to seeing it in a moment, so I won't keep you for too long," Mrs. Hamilton continued. "And of course there's the outreach program."

Ruth nudged me, while Sara turned and sneered.

"Yes. The outreach program, which I believe got off to a . . . how can I put this? A . . . *hair-raising* start, but there are plans to keep it developing, and I do hope that more of you will be inspired to take part. Now. To the awards. It's always been the tradition at Avebury to give praise where it's due, encouragement where it's deserved, and admonishment where it's needed. I can't say how pleased I am to be here this year to give out these awards personally. It's one of the perks of being one of the school's benefactors. So let's get started. The first award goes to the student who has done the best academically so far, and that goes to Sophie Johnson in the eleventh grade. Well done, and come forward, Sophie."

A dark-haired girl I didn't know made her way forward to the stage and was given a huge box of chocolates and an iPod.

"Well done," said Mrs. Hamilton as she shook Sophie's hand. "Now, for heaven's sake, lighten up and get a life, girl. Chill out a bit. A happy life means a balance between hard work *and* pleasure."

Everyone looked at each other in amazement, especially the parents. This wasn't like the awards ceremonies at my old school.

"Next," said Mrs. Hamilton. "An award for the most lazy girl in school. Maisie Pickford, come forward."

Maisie Pickford turned bright red but made her way up onto the stage, where she was given an armful of books.

"And you, young lady. You have a brain," said Mrs. Hamilton. "Now use it."

A few sophomores started laughing.

"Okay, who's next?" asked Mrs. Hamilton. "Oh, yes. The next award is for the student who has shown the most promise this term."

At the front, Sara smoothed back her hair and had another scratch.

"This is the one that I think Sara's after," whispered Ruth.

"And the winner is . . . Gemma Whiting," called Mrs. Hamilton.

"Omigod!" I exclaimed. "That's me."

Ruth beamed at me and pushed me off my chair and toward the stage, where, moments later, I climbed up and stood next to a smiling Mrs. Hamilton.

"I've chosen Gemma for this award," she said, "because she's only been here one term, and despite a difficult start, she's made excellent progress—and no thanks to many of you in this room, according to what I've heard from Mrs. Blain and some of the other teachers. It's hard changing schools in eighth grade when you're not beginning together and not all in the same boat. In the future, I'm going to ask all of you to be more sensitive to the people around you who are new or don't know the ropes as well as you do, and that goes for the parents and friends here tonight, too, whatever the situation you're in. Don't be selfish. Give out the hand of friendship, or else . . . you'll have me to answer to, and I may be old, but I can be tough!"

A cheer came from the right, and I looked over to see that it had come from Hermie, who was grinning up at Mrs. Hamilton.

She beamed back at him. "As you know, a lot of the money raised this year will go toward building the new science lab. But I thought of something else I'd like to see developed here. I'm going to have a new wing built for the outreach program, where anyone who wants to can go on Friday afternoons and train in various skills. I'm going to invite all of the leading experts in their fields to come and talk to you. You can train to do beauty so that you can take those skills with you into hospitals and nursing homes . . . *and*," she said and gave me a huge smile at this point, "I will invite some of the experts from some animal-therapy programs in

172

so that you can learn about taking in animals."

At the mention of the word "animals," a soft groan came from the front row. I looked down and got the feeling that it was Sara who had made the noise. She was certainly looking unhappy.

"Gemma was quite right in her idea that animals can give tremendous comfort to the old, the infirm, the lonely," Mrs. Hamilton continued. "In fact, I've already hired an expert in that field, and he's going to be here at the start of next term. All of this was inspired by the girl standing here in front of you. She wanted to make a difference, and I'd like you all to learn from her. And because of that, I'm going to call the program the Gemma Whiting Project."

I felt myself turning bright red, but Mrs. Hamilton hadn't finished.

"Now, I know I'm an old lady, and you probably all think I'm a bit batty, but I can tell you one thing. There's nothing more miserable in this life than being lonely and feeling left out. People feel it at school. People feel it at work. People feel it when they're old. Be aware and do what you can. Take a little time out from thinking about yourself all the time. There's a lot of suffering in the world, and it's not all in faraway places. Be aware of what's happening around you. On your doorstep. In your home, your neighborhood, your school."

Everyone in the hall looked at each other and then back at the stage, and then a cheer went up, this time from some juniors and seniors in the back rows. Soon the rest of the hall joined in with them. Rose, Grace, Imogen, Ruth, and Tasha were all grinning and giving me the thumbs-up. I could hardly believe what was happening.

"Would you like to say something, Gemma?" asked Mrs. Hamilton.

I shook my head, but she nudged me toward the podium.

I took a deep breath and looked out at the sea of faces in front of me.

"I . . . I didn't want to come here at first," I said. "And it's true, I found my first few weeks hard, that first month, in fact, but . . . but, well, if my time here has shown me anything, it's that, as Mrs. Hamilton said, life *is* a roller coaster. Up and down. New challenges, new obstacles. I've learned never to give up, because you never know what the future holds and what each new day will bring. Um. That's all, I think."

A cheer rose again from the back of the hall, and I looked out to see rows of smiling faces. Except for Sara's, that is. She looked very strange. Like someone had blown her up with a bicycle pump. Her lips were swollen, her eyes were bulging out of their sockets, her face was covered in ugly red blotches and sweat, and her hair had come out of its immaculate bun and was sticking all over her face like wet straw. And she was clawing at her face like it was on fire.

"Oh, my. Oh, dear. Oh, heck," cried Mrs. Woods, getting to her feet when she saw Sara fall to her knees and start groaning. "Quick, someone, get the nurse! Get the doctor!"

It seemed like everything went into fast gear. The school nurse and the doctor were called and rushed to the front. Someone brought a bowl of water and began splashing Sara's face. I got down from the stage and went back to join Ruth. An ambulance was called. Guests were ushered off into the dining area for preshow drinks, and Mrs. Woods started dancing around like she had ants in her pants, trying to get the rest of the cast backstage.

A stretcher was brought from the clinic, and four juniors picked up Sara and laid her on it. They carried her down the aisle, with the doctor and nurse following behind. Just as they reached where Ruth, Tasha, and I were sitting, Sara peered out at me through bulging, toadlike eyes. She looked awful. Nothing like the pretty girl she was. She looked like a monster. She raised a swollen finger and pointed. "All your fault," she moaned as she was carried off.

"*Me?* What did I do?" I asked the others.

"Nothing," said Tasha, stepping forward and

linking my arm. "Take no notice. I think I know *exactly* what's happened. She's allergic to animals. That boa around her neck was the real thing. Genuine ostrich feathers."

"Allergic to animals?" Ruth repeated. "Omigod! Bertie!"

"Bertie?" I asked. "What's he got to do with it?"

"Remember that day your dad brought him and I found him?"

"Yeah. So?"

"Do you remember *where* I found him?"

"Um . . . oh! Yes. In the drama department!"

"In the *props* room to be precise, and now that I remember, he was curled up very comfortably on a pale pink boa."

"And come to think of it, Boris the cat likes to sneak in there for a nap, too. I've seen him a few times. It's next to the boiler room, so it's cozy. Feathers *and* dog and cat hair! No wonder she had an allergic reaction."

"But will she be all right?" I asked. "She looked terrible."

Tasha nodded. "Not in time for the show, but she'll be fine as soon as they've given her an antiallergy shot. Same thing happened last summer when she came to stay with my family and our cat slept on her pillow one afternoon when we'd gone out. She blew up like a balloon when she got into bed later that night."

Ruth started giggling.

"What's so funny?" I asked.

"She said it was your fault, and well . . . you *are* the Lady of the Beasts," she said and then put on a spooky voice. "Beeeeewaaaaare the Lady of the Beasts. Her power must never be unleeeeeeeashed, or eeeeeelse she will sic her dog on you."

Tasha started laughing, too. "She did look awful, didn't she?" she said. "And I know I shouldn't laugh, but she'll be okay, really she will . . . But in the meantime, she's turned from a goddess to a geek. Serves her right. I hope someone took a picture of her."

At that moment, Mrs. Woods came flying into the hall and looked around frantically.

"Gemma, Gemma," she called.

I raced over.

"You're on. Five minutes. Oh, my. Oh, dear. Oh, heck. The show must go on."

"Me? On? And do what?"

"Tallulah, of course," said Mrs. Woods as she beckoned me to the backstage area. "You're the only one who knows the part besides Sara!"

Behind her, I saw Hermie leaning against a pillar. He looked over at me and winked.

And so I got to play out my fantasy. All of those days memorizing Tallulah's words and driving Mom and

Dad crazy finally paid off as I took center stage. The show was a terrific success. I gave it my all and had the most amazing time ever, and afterward everyone said that it was one of the best shows that the school had ever put on. As I got changed back into my school uniform, Mrs. Woods took me aside and said that I had "saved the day."

After the show was over, the guests began to drift out toward the parking lot, and I walked Mrs. Hamilton out to the front to say thank you and goodbye.

"Where's your car?" I asked as I looked around the courtyard for her Rolls Royce.

"Oh, I sent it on," she said as a familiar figure roared up the driveway on his motorcycle.

A few seconds later, Hermie pulled up beside us.

He winked at me. "Had a good evening?" he asked with a grin.

"The best," I said and smiled back.

Hermie then pulled a helmet out of the box on the back of his bike. I thought he was going to hand it to me and ask me to go for a ride, but he gave it to Mrs. Hamilton.

"Your carriage awaits, madam," he said.

She blushed and, for a moment, looked like a coy teenager. She put on the helmet and hoisted herself up on the back of his bike with surprising agility, and then she put her arms around Hermie's waist.

"Hang in there, Zodiac Girl," she said and smiled at me.

"You, too, Z. G.," I said and smiled back.

"And I'll be watching out for you," said Hermie as he revved up his engine. "Just don't forget—the magic's all around you, Gemma, inside and out. Make the most of it. It's your choice what you do with it. But, for now, it's over and out."

"Yes, sir," I said with a salute.

And, with that, they roared off down the driveway and out of sight.

The Gemini Files
Characteristics, Facts, and Fun

May 22—June 21

Whether it's chatting on their cell phones, gossiping with their friends, or firing off e-mails, Geminis are great communicators, and they love to talk, talk, talk! Persuasion is their middle name, and they often charm people in order to get their way. They are multifaceted, strong willed, and independent.

Geminis push themselves to the max with their sense of adventure and fun, but, as a result, they can end up biting off more than they can chew. This can lead to confusion—but that's not surprising, as their star symbol is the twins—showing a dual personality.

Element:	Air
Color:	Yellow, silver
Birthstone:	Emerald/agate
Animal:	Magpie
Lucky day:	Wednesday
Planet:	Ruled by Mercury

Gemini's best friends are likely to be:
Aries
Gemini
Sagittarius
Aquarius

Gemini's enemies are likely to be:
Scorpio
Taurus

A Gemini's idea of heaven would be:
Hosting their own prime-time talk show.

A Gemini would go crazy if:
They were grounded without their phone
and computer.

Nessa's Top Makeover Tips

1. **Accentuate your best feature!** It will draw attention away from those features you don't like as much.

2. **Love your hair!** It's fun to straighten your hair if it's curly, or curl it if it's straight, but it's much better to make the best of it as it is.

3. **Bring out your eyes!** If you have green eyes, purple eye shadow will make them look greener, and green makes blue eyes sparkle. Blue is great for brown eyes.

4. **Try a new hair color!** Get a friend to help you dye

your hair using semipermanent color for a whole new look! (Check with your parents first, though.)

5. **Neat nails!** Keep your nails looking neat and paint them a fun color—it will brighten your day!

6. **Mags rule!** Look through magazines to find a look you like, and copy it!

Are you a typical Gemini?

It's the weekend! What are you planning to do?
A) Shopping, plain and simple.
B) Anything, as long as it's outdoors!
C) Reading and writing in your journal.

You're planning a vacation with some friends. What kind of break do you choose?
A) Relaxing by the pool, somewhere hot, so you can work on your suntan.
B) Something sporty, like skiing. You love being active.
C) Somewhere with lots of interesting history, where you can learn and explore.

What's your favorite subject at school?
A) You hate them all except dance and drama, where you can show off.
B) English is your favorite by far – you have a way with words.
C) Honestly, you like them all. You really like learning new things.

You're going to a party and you need to look fabulous. What outfit do you choose?

A) Something simple, a black dress maybe.

B) Lots of bright colors—you like to stand out in a crowd.

C) Your outfits are always a mixture of many different styles, patterns, and colors.

What do you get into trouble for most at school?

A) Being late—you take so long to get ready in the morning and you lose track of time.

B) Chatting and gossiping. You love to talk, even during class!

C) You never get into trouble. Teacher's pet? *Toi?*

You have a French exchange student staying with you and her English is terrible. What do you do?

A) Ignore her. You have better things to do with your time than hang out with her.

B) Use the international language of mime to get your point across. So what if you look silly?

C) Chatter away to her in French, of course. You don't care what language it is, as long as you get to communicate.

How did you score?

Mostly As—gentle Gemini
Are you sure you're a Gemini? Get gossiping!

Mostly Bs—gorgeous Gemini
Hmm, it sounds like your Gemini side is fighting to get out. Set it free!

Mostly Cs—gabby Gemini
Chatty and outgoing, you're Gemini from head to toe.

Zodiac Girls by Cathy Hopkins

Every month a Zodiac Girl is chosen, and for that month the planets give her advice. When will *your* sign shine?

Brat Princess
Leo

Dancing Queen
Aries

Discount Diva
Taurus

Recipe for Rebellion
Sagittarius

Star Child
Virgo